tastes like SUGAR

BECCA SEYMOUR

RAINBOW TREE PUBLISHING

ALSO BY BECCA SEYMOUR

ZONE DEFENSE

NO TAKE BACKS | NO MORE SECRETS | NO WRONG MOVES
| NO BACKING DOWN

FAST BREAK

RULES, SCHMULES! | FACTS, SMACTS! | REGULAR SMEGULAR!
| EASY, SCHMEASY!

TRUE-BLUE

LET ME SHOW YOU | I'VE GOT YOU | BECOMING US |
THINKING IT OVER | ALWAYS FOR YOU | IT'S NOT YOU |
OUR FIRST & LAST | NEXT FOR US

OUTBACK BOYS

STUMBLE | BOUNCE | WOBBLE

FANGS & FELONS

THICKER THAN WATER | WEAKER THAN INSTINCT |
BRIGHTER THAN FEAR | STRONGER THAN FATE

STAND-ALONE CONTEMPORARY

NOT USED TO CUTE | HIGH ALERT | REALIGNED |
AMALGAMATED | UNDER THE BLAZING STARS | BEST KIND
OF AWKWARD | TASTES LIKE SUGAR

For information, contact the author: hello@beccaseymour.com

EDITING: HOT TREE EDITING

COVER DESIGNER: ETHEREAL DESIGNS

PUBLISHER: RAINBOW TREE PUBLISHING

PAPERBACK ISBN: 978-1-923252-10-3

CHAPTER ONE

SULLY

I ACCEPT my second beer with a grateful smile. "Thanks."

"All good. Are you ready to order?"

I cast another brief glance at the menu, the name *Jake's Tap* sprawled on the top. It's fairly limited, but from the plates I've seen brought out of the kitchen, everything looks and smells incredible. "I'll grab the burger and homemade fries, please."

"Good choice. It won't be long." The bartender offers me an up-nod before he heads away to take another order. I track his movements for a few seconds simply as something to do, a distraction more than anything deeper.

Not that he isn't attractive, but I'm pretty sure he's got something going with the guy propping up the other end of the bar. The dark-haired man has barely taken his gaze off the bartender. The times he has, it's to shoot people the stink eye.

Getting on someone's shit list, especially since I need to decide whether to accept the job offer in this small country town, is the last thing I want. Collier's Creek, from what I've seen and from the stories my sister's told me, is pretty close-knit.

All it takes is one asshole to spin bullshit that makes the world you've built come tumbling down. Life has taught me that. The asshole I'm referring to is my ex, who's also someone I used to work with.

The moral of *that* particular story is don't mix work with pleasure. Okay, so there's a second moral too. That one is don't fall for pricks who think it's fun to make false promises, offer you a ring and commitment, only to then fall on someone else's dick the very same day.

Add in a steady buildup of gaslighting and *ding, ding, ding,* we have a winner.

Talk about a wake-up call.

At forty-seven, I'm over the bullshit. Over the drama.

I'm over big-city living, which is the reason six months after all that went down in San Francisco, I clung to my sister's suggestion to stay in the small studio above her garage in this ridiculously cute town until I figured things out.

After just eight days, I scored a job interview and an offer that actually has me excited. Truthfully, I don't really have that much to think about. The position feels serendipitous.

For one, as the only administrator—technically the office manager—I won't get caught up in dick-measuring contests or have to live with my guard up to protect myself from backstabbers. This is a giant drawcard. The second is one that completely blew my mind. While the initial interview was conducted by the lead administrator, Jeremy, from the government office in Cheyenne, and the person I would be replacing—a woman called Marge who's desperate to retire—the captain of the Collier's Creek fire station was then brought in. Since I'd be directly working for them, under their command, it made sense.

And the mind-blown part?

Captain Zoey Jackson. When she'd stepped into the room, I'd done a double take, as did Marge and Jeremy when Zoey gave me a giant hug.

The world is a funny place and sometimes a small one.

While Zoey hadn't lived in San Francisco for

long, our paths had crossed during the Pride parade about ten or so years back, and we'd been good friends until we'd lost touch when she'd moved away. To Collier's Creek, apparently.

And for the first time in what seems like years, I feel like I can take in a lungful of air and truly breathe. That alone tells me I'd been treading water in SF and had become tired of the game before I'd been ready to admit it.

Sure, Collier's Creek has clean air, and the town's idea of god-awful traffic is when three cars have to wait one minute when a moose decides to cross the road, gets spooked, and rams a pickup truck before bolting—which legit happened three days ago. But there's more to it than my ability to breathe better.

I take a long pull of my beer, appreciating the crisp tang.

Laughter catches my attention, and a smile tugs at my lips when I see a burly man dot a sweet kiss on another guy's forehead before he holds his hand.

Yeah, this place is helping to cleanse my soul or something. I think I need that.

The "Hey, Tad" directed at the bartender from my other side surprises me.

I jerk and grab hold of the bar top to stop myself

from falling off my stool. A warm hand on my arm stops the final wobble.

"Shit, you okay?" the man with the deep voice asks.

I relax my grip and release a soft chuckle. "Almost got me." I turn toward the younger guy at my side. As I do, he releases me, leaving a trace of warmth behind. My gaze lands on a smiling mouth, the smirk a little crooked, as though he's not sure if he should be concerned or laughing with me. I flick my attention farther up, my mouth turning instantly dry at the thirst trap of a man before me.

Thirst trap? Jesus, is that even what people say anymore? Hell, perhaps they never even did. Thank fuck mind-reading abilities don't exist. If they did, his crooked smile that's becoming more amused by my wide-eyed stare definitely wouldn't be directed my way.

A guy like this, all wide shoulders, broad chest, and a full head of hair that's many years away from receding, wouldn't even entertain the possibility of—

I stop myself short. The last thing I need to do is think about sex while in a bar full of strangers. Sure, if this were a club and that were the scene, I would drink my fill. But this bar definitely isn't that.

What this *is* is him still staring at me.

"Yeah, I'm good. Thanks for the save," I respond quickly, figuring he's just waiting for me to remember how to speak after eyeing him for so long.

"That's a relief."

"One burger and fries."

My gaze snaps to the same bartender and then to the plate of food that he sets down. "Thanks."

"All good. There's a booth that just opened if you want to grab it," Tad offers, dipping his head in the direction behind me.

"Oh." I angle that way and realize no one else is eating at the bar. "Sure, thanks." I pick up my plate as Tad focuses on the guy who I'm sure rarely eats a pile of grease-filled food. And if he did, from the way his muscles fill out his long-sleeved T-shirt, I suspect he spends an unholy amount of time in the gym.

"Hayes, what'll it be?"

Hayes. I risk a glance at him, finding his attention on me before I look away and head to the open booth. That has to be his last name, right? Back when I was a teenager, my friends used to call me Sully. Sure, Tom's a solid name, but my younger self thought shortening my last name from Sullivan to Sully was the coolest thing ever.

That nickname was quickly ousted by corporate when I got my first job.

I settle in the booth, wondering when it was I became so white collar and why, oh fucking why, I thought I enjoyed the rat race.

In the three different companies I worked for over the years, I was far from the top dog, nor was I a seven-figure executive like one of my previous bosses. But at some point, I'd bought into the whole fast-paced world, where it was all about who you wore and who you fucked and who you could get ahead of.

The friendly chatter drifting around me is nothing like I've experienced in the last few years. It's not even like I have anyone to blame for that other than myself.

Not taking the job here would be foolish. The more I think about it, the more certain I am.

It's less money than I've earned in years, almost a quarter less, in fact, but I'm also lucky that I bought a condo when I was just twenty-five—with the support of my parents—and sold it for a profit (thanks to the crazy house-price increase over the past twenty years), which takes the pressure off.

Mom inherited a house from her great-aunt, and because I have kick-ass parents (both are thankfully enjoying life in a retirement village a town over, having moved to be closer to my sister in their golden years), they split the funds from the sale of the house between me and my sister. Hence the reason I was lucky enough to afford a place in San Francisco and sell it so quickly a couple of weeks back.

I take a big bite of my burger. With light spices and tender beef, the combination is delicious. As is the grease I should really be trying to avoid.

Tomorrow morning, I'll make sure I go for a walk. A run would be better, but the last time I ran, I was in my twenties, and even then, it was probably because I was late for work. My jeans have jumped up at least two sizes since then, and while I'm not 100 percent okay with that, it's something I made peace with years ago.

Or as much as a guy can when in the company of fitter men.

But I really should be more heart-aware—at least according to my sister. Despite that, I take another bite of the burger, my shoulders relaxing at the flavor and the overall contentment over a successful day.

A presence has me pausing from taking another bite. My gaze lands on the same broad chest I spent a little too long admiring earlier before it travels higher.

Those same bright, slightly amused twinkling eyes meet mine.

"Mind if I join you?"

My brows shoot high.

"It's busy tonight. Thought it would make sense to fill up the empty seat if that's okay?"

"Sure," I say with a nod, taking Hayes in as he places his thick jacket on the padded bench before settling his tall frame in. I return his smile, then have no clue what to do next.

Do I just take another huge mouthful of my burger, or do I make polite conversation? During the past six months—even before that, if I'm honest with myself—I've been a bit hermit-like. But being tired of the scene, tired of being taken for a fool by my ex, who lied when he said he wanted a monogamous relationship, meant moments like this—a couple of beers and a burger in a bar—were me having a "big night."

"Please, don't let your food go cold. Tad's bringing me the same meal in—Here he is now."

Tad places the piled plate, complete with a basket of onion rings, on the table. "Enjoy," he says before returning straight back to the bar.

This Hayes guy wasn't exaggerating about how full Jake's Tap is. This is the first time I've been, so I have no idea if this is normal for a Thursday night or not.

"Thanks, Tad," Hayes calls to the bartender's retreating form, pulling my attention back to him. "The name's Hayes." He reaches out.

I quickly place my burger down, wipe my hands on the napkin, and shake his hand. "Sully." The name's out before I second-guess or even question it.

His smile brightens. "Good to meet you. Now"—he indicates toward my food—"don't hold back on my account." Unceremoniously, he picks up his burger and takes a large bite. I follow suit.

"I haven't seen you in Jake's before," he says after swallowing his mouthful of food.

I shake my head. "First time here."

"It was a good choice for food. The menu's fairly simple, but I've never not had a good feed here." He smiles before chewing on a fry.

"Well, this burger's definitely hitting the spot."

He nods before saying, "You're not from around here, then? Just passing through?"

"No, and I'm not too sure yet."

Hayes studies me, his gaze roaming my face before dipping lower. My brows shoot high. Is he checking me out? Straight guys don't look at other men quite this way.

Heat forms in my stomach. I let it simmer, not wanting to douse the flame of possibility just yet.

Will I be disappointed if I'm setting myself up for rejection? Maybe a little, but also fuck it.

Today's been such a good day—why not push my luck a little and see where it gets me? A cock in my mouth or my ass are pretty spectacular options.

When his attention returns to my face and he reads my expression, a smirk forms. There's zero embarrassment at being caught out. The sexier his smile grows, the more I'm sure he's definitely checking me out.

"A man of mystery and one who's happy to go with the flow…. We could do with a little more of that around here."

"Is that right?" I tilt my head, and this time, I'm the one dipping my gaze, eating up the expanse of his broad chest before reconnecting with his sparkling eyes.

He seriously is a good-looking guy, and he appears to like what he sees. Mama didn't raise no fool. I was taught long ago not to look a gift horse in the mouth.

"Absolutely. An attractive guy possibly sticking

around. Or maybe he'll be leaving in the winter's breeze in a day or two…. Either way, it's important you get the best Collier's Creek welcome going."

A laugh breaks free between us. I shake my head in amusement, appreciating that Hayes doesn't take himself too seriously.

"And you're the best welcome?" I tease.

"Good food, good company…." He shrugs, taking another bite, leaving his words, which I'm totally interpreting as an offer, hanging.

We continue eating, chatting about TV shows and movies, music and sports, and nothing of deep significance. While our music tastes are leagues apart, the fact that he's rewatched *Ted* almost as many times as I have makes me smile.

When I finally finish my burger, I pick up one of my fries.

"You're one of those eaters, huh?"

I freeze with a fry touching my lips, gaze snapping to his. "Excuse me?" I pull the fry away. Our meal so far has been easy, companionable even. That it's not been deep or personal, I've liked a lot. That he's commenting on how I eat…. Yeah, that's not going to—

"You eat each type of food separately rather than mixing it up." From the speed of his answer, I've little doubt he heard the guarded surprise in my question. His slightly widened eyes are a dead give-away too. He points at his plate. "I like to mix it up."

I glance down. He's polished off half of his fries and almost all of his burger.

Shit.

This is also why being a hermit over the past few years has suited me. Though, he's done an impressive job at reminding me how, with the right person, it's easy to be sociable and myself.

At work, I get into the mindset of the job and hold my own with ease. You have to in administration, especially if you don't want to be walked over, but fuck, I hate that I've become oversensitive, prepared to defend myself. I never used to be this guy.

Aware I've made things awkward as hell, I force a smile. "Yeah." That's all I have. Any second now, Hayes, who, let's face it, is no doubt wishing he'd found another place to sit, is going to stand up and leave.

Probably call Tad ahead of time before coming back to Jake's Tap, checking I'm not here and that it's safe to return.

"I had a roommate who used to do that," he says immediately. His shoulders relax, and he picks up a fry and pops it into his mouth with a smile, completely ignoring the awkwardness. When he's finished chewing, he continues, "He used to have a thing about his food groups touching. In the end, I found one of those split plate things. I don't know what they're called. They remind me a little of the old-school trays in elementary school."

"A divided plate, so each section's portioned off?" I pick up my beer and take a sip, happy he hasn't run off.

"Yeah. They had a whole range. Metal, plastic, different colors. Phil—that was the guy's name— thought it was awesome." He takes a bite of his burger, seeming happy when I pick up a fry, following my movement with a smile.

Admittedly, his story, however random, is pretty sweet. That he'd do that rather than ridicule his friend says a lot about him.

"I don't have issues with food touching." I shrug. "I just eat the best bits of food first."

He nods. "So if you get full, it doesn't matter if you leave the rest."

I chuckle. "That's the reason. Though, to be fair, I can polish off a meal this size with no issues." I rub my gut for good measure. Over the years, I've learned it's easier if I draw attention to my thick waist. I know I'm not obese according to those depressing BMI charts, but I'm definitely overweight.

Hayes tracks my movement, but rather than laughing with me, which is the usual response I get, he tilts his head, and his brow furrows. Flicking his attention back to my face, he seems to study me a beat.

Heat gathers in my chest, and I try hard to shove away the impending embarrassment.

"In that case, do you have room for dessert?"

I part my lips but stop short of speaking, his expression halting me.

Deep brown eyes are fixed on me. There's no amusement or derision in sight.

Holy shit. Does he mean *dessert* dessert?

"I have a pint of unopened ice cream at my place. It's just five minutes away. Both the ice cream and my house." His gaze doesn't waver.

"I'm allergic to tree nuts" tumbles out of my mouth. Immediately, I want to take the words back. Maybe even cover my face.

His lips twitch. "I'll keep the maple syrup and pecan ice cream sealed, in that case."

I swallow hard, my cock thickening at the very thought of going home with Hayes. I dip the tip of my tongue out and swipe it over my bottom lip. "And when you say ice cream…?"

Leaning forward, he reaches out and ghosts his fingers over my forearm. My goose bumps are immediate. They intensify when he lowers his voice and says, "That's exactly the plan. I want to see how quickly I can make you scream."

Fuck.

A shudder weaves its way through me, and I'm nodding fast and hard and probably looking like a bobblehead. "Yeah, okay." Damn, the man's pickup game is strong. And I'm here for it.

He eases back in the booth, picks up a fry, and pops it into his mouth. "Let me settle up at the bar and we'll go. Unless you want to finish your fries."

"No." I clear my throat, trying to calm down my eagerness. "I'm good to leave now."

"Perfect." He combines his response with a rake of his gaze over my face. I feel its journey. My cheeks flush, and I swear the heat in his eyes deepens. When he stands, I track his movements, my body vibrating with need.

Jesus H. Christ.

I take a calming breath, finish off my beer, then stand. This is not how I saw my night going. My lips twitch. Staying in Collier's Creek permanently is looking sweeter and sweeter.

He's back before I know it, and I realize I've let him pay. "Shit." I tug out my wallet. "What do I owe you?"

He shakes his head. "My treat."

"You didn't need to do that." That he did unfurls more heat in my stomach.

"I wanted to," he says, indicating the door with a nod as he tugs on his coat.

"Thanks," I offer, not quite sure when the last time was a guy bought me a meal.

We step out into the quiet street, the cool breeze whipping by us. "Fuck, it's cold."

Hayes's chuckle is soft. "If you do stick around, just wait until the snow comes."

I tug my jacket around me, wishing I had a hat and scarf. It's something I really need to invest in. Maybe a giant sleeping-bag coat, too, which is a thing I saw on a sketchy website, so I know they exist. Though, knowing my luck, I'll order it and end up with a miniature one made for a Ken doll or something.

"My place is south of town. I've just had one light beer, so are you okay if I drive us?"

"Sounds good," I say gratefully, not having

thought that far ahead. No way could I have brought Hayes back to my sister's. Talk about sketchy.

Hayes's shoulder brushes mine as we head down the street and toward his vehicle. Not only is his heat welcome, but he's sticking close and clinging to the connection we felt at the bar.

"This is me."

We stop outside an old pickup truck. It's not souped-up, and it needs some TLC. It's also not what I expected.

"Nice truck."

He pauses from getting in the driver's seat, his gaze meeting mine. I see the question there and am sure he's wondering if I'm mocking him. That's the furthest thing from the truth.

I like that he doesn't have something flashy. Not a vehicle that's all about image and bling or whatever kids these days are driving.

"It's about the same age I am," I offer with a chuckle. There's no hiding that there's a clear disparity in our ages. "It brings back fond memories. My uncle used to have one."

He sends a beaming smile my way, and when he gets in, I settle beside him, grinning at the well-worn bench seat.

It takes a couple of tries to get the engine started,

and while I'm pretty sure pink dusts his cheeks, the whole setup and his reaction are endearing. I like being surprised.

It finally gets going, and he pulls away from the curb, saying, "It's a Ford F-100. It used to be my pops's." His voice takes on a softer tone, and I wince, pretty sure I know where he's going with this story.

"Pops bought it brand new in '75," Hayes continues, glancing over at me with a grin that's a mix of pride and nostalgia. "Man, you should see him now. He's eighty and still driving his old Harley around town like he's twenty. Last Christmas, he put on a Santa suit and rode around handing out candy canes. Ended up in a snowbank 'cause he insisted on doing donuts in the church parking lot."

I burst out laughing, imagining an old man in a Santa suit causing chaos on a Harley. "He sounds like a riot."

"Oh, he's something else." Hayes nods. "Last summer, he convinced the whole family to go on this wild goose chase to find 'Bigfoot.' We ended up camping in the woods for a week, Pops swearing up and down he saw something 'real suspicious' every night. Turned out he was just messing with us—had a costume and everything. Scared the living daylights outta my cousin Joe."

I'm laughing so hard that tears prick my eyes. "Jesus, here I was thinking my dad was a handful when he glued all the remote controls together so we'd have more 'family time.' And yes, when I was a teenager, we had remote controls and everything. It was the most exciting thing to be invented before DVDs."

Hayes snorts and shakes his head.

"But your pops sounds like he's on another level."

Hayes chuckles, navigating a turn. "Yeah, he's a trip. Keeps everyone on their toes."

We continue down the road, passing quaint storefronts and quiet streets, a happy warmth drifting between us. Am I still horny? Fuck yes. I'm sporting a semi, but the laughter between us is refreshing.

Turning the blinker on, Hayes glances at me, a wide smile aimed my way. "This is me."

I look out the window and take in the small bungalow. Light spills onto the front porch from the lantern next to the door. "Nice place."

Hayes's fidgeting draws my attention back to him. He seems self-conscious.

"It's not much, but it's mine, you know?"

Surprise has me furrowing my brow. What on earth does he have to be embarrassed by? "It looks great. I imagine property prices here have gone crazy, as have rentals."

"It's not as bad as other places, but it's pricy. I bought this fixer-upper a couple of years back. It's just one bed, one bath—"

"It looks solid, and as you said, it's yours. Which already makes me think that it's a good place."

"Yeah?" His eyes brighten.

This man, he's fucking irresistible. So far, he's taken the lead, so this hint of vulnerability is unexpected. I'm not going to lie and say I don't like it.

"How about," I say as I unbuckle myself, "you let me in, and I can see for myself?" I lean toward him, and he immediately takes the hint.

Hayes closes the distance between us, pressing his lips to mine with an unexpected tenderness. The kiss is soft, almost hesitant, as if we're both testing the waters. The warmth of his breath, the slight quiver of his lips as they meet mine—I savor each sensation.

He cups my cheek, thumb brushing my skin gently, sending shivers down my spine. At his touch, the kiss deepens, drawing a soft gasp and a shuddering breath from me as our tongues brush.

Fuck, I want him.

Hayes is intoxicating, drawing me in with every passing second.

My palm finds its way to the back of his neck, tangling my fingers in his hair as I pull him closer.

"Inside," he gasps, tugging us apart.

"Me," I state, not the trace of a quiver in my voice, feeling bold with the firmness of my cock and the intensity of our kiss. "I want you inside me."

"Fuck." The word punches out of him.

Rather than going in for another kiss, Hayes shoves open his door, clasps my hand, and draws me out his side of the pickup.

Thank you, Ford, for the ease of bench seats.

He doesn't stop, completely on a mission to get us inside his home. I'm on board, meeting him stride for stride. That he doesn't need to unlock the door, just opens the damn thing, probably deserves a question about home safety, but I'm too desperate to care.

I don't have time to take in the living space because Hayes's palm against mine is firm, his stride unrelenting until we're in his bedroom.

"Clothes." He punctuates the growled demand with a heated kiss.

I don't have time to grasp onto him or start

humping his damn leg before he breaks the kiss to tug his coat off, then his long-sleeved tee.

But I can't move, can barely remember how to breathe as I drink him in.

An expanse of skin is revealed, so toned and sculpted that my lips part. Wide-eyed, I stare. I've never seen a body so defined in real life before. Not even in my youth.

"Fuck, your body…."

The corners of his lips lift high, cockiness filling his features that's all self-confidence and certainty rather than arrogance. "Is going to fuck you so damn good." He steps into my space, his unzipped jeans revealing a splatter of pubic hair that I'm keen to rub my face against.

Before I can respond to his dirty-as-fuck words, he tugs off my jacket, pulls off my sweater, and unceremoniously removes my T-shirt. A flicker of unease pulses in my gut. We're so different. Our age, our shapes and sizes, my—

Any uncertainty cuts off when he latches on to my nipple, nibbling and licking as he grips my ass with firm hands and squeezes.

My cock punches against my jeans, and I cling to him, dropping my head back and allowing myself to enjoy his warm mouth.

"I can't wait to taste you," he murmurs as he kisses his way to my other nipple and moves one of his hands to my groin. He squeezes lightly, pulling a gasp from me. "You're going to stretch my mouth fucking perfectly."

I groan when he squeezes again, barely registering how smooth and hot his skin feels under my wandering hands.

His mouth on me will have me coming too fast, and there's not a chance I'll be able to go again quickly. Hell, I can't remember the last time I came more than once in a night. Even twice in a week without my own hand.

The thought has me tugging Hayes up and capturing his mouth.

I want him inside me. Want him to remind me how phenomenal it feels to get railed when fueled by lust and passion.

Everything about Hayes screams sex and fun and desire.

I need that now.

He plunges his tongue into my mouth, and I shiver in need.

I pull away, my heart speeding up when he chases me for more. "Lube?" I ask between his kisses. "Where's your lube?"

He grunts and kisses me once, twice, and a third time before gripping my waist and urging me onto his bed. I sit willingly, kicking off my shoes and focusing on undressing as quickly as possible. The whole time, I keep my attention on him as he moves to his bedside cabinet.

He breaks eye contact, taking in my now-naked body.

I wait for the discomfort to kick in, but the lust in Hayes's eyes doesn't give me the chance to overthink.

He wants me—maybe even as much as I want him.

"You're good to bottom, right?" he asks, voice dipping low as he tugs off his jeans. His cock springs free, long and uncut. It's hard to look away as I imagine going down on him, playing with his foreskin. "Sully."

My eyes snap up, and I meet his gaze. His brows are pulled up in question and amusement.

"Yes." I nod.

"Thank fuck. I didn't want to assume, but based on what you said earlier…."

I have no clue what I said earlier. All I can think about is his big dick, his perfect body, and the way he makes me feel sexy.

When he's fully naked, he kneels on the bed with a smile. "You want to move back and let me take care of you?"

Fuck yes, I do.

I scramble back, head landing on the soft pillow that smells like him. It's an aftershave I don't recognize and his natural scent that's woodsy and fresh. I consider turning my head farther into the pillow and inhaling deeply, but Hayes's hand on my thigh leaves me trembling and aching.

"You're so fucking sexy."

My gaze snaps to his.

Everything from his gravelly tone to the intensity in his deep brown gaze tells me all I need to know.

He's serious and he wants me.

"Even sexier when your dick's inside me," I challenge, the passion in his gaze bolstering me.

He's quick to laugh. "I have no doubt you're right."

"Condom?"

He reveals the packet in his hand I hadn't seen. "I'm on PrEP and negative. Regular checks, but—"

"Me too," I'm quick to say. "I'm good to give that a miss if you are."

With a smirk that's all satisfaction and promise, he throws the condom on the floor.

The click of the lube bottle sounds loud. Tension hums through my veins, encouraging me to ease back and bend my knees. I spread my legs wide after planting my feet, then hesitate.

Maybe he wants me on my knees. Maybe—

"Just like that. Fuck, look at your hole." A swallow follows, loud in the otherwise quiet room. "I'm going to stretch you so good."

At the first touch, my eyes roll into the back of my head. His thick fingers drive into me, probing, careful to ease me open. He offers me sporadic kisses on my lips, my chest, my extra-sensitive nipples, working me up and taking care of me until I'm panting and writhing, asking for his cock.

"Hayes, fuck, I'm ready."

A salacious grin forms as he rises and stares down at me. "You are, huh?"

"The three fingers in my ass say yes."

His chuckle is loud. I grin even as he strokes against my prostrate and I arch up, squeezing his digits.

"In that case, I better not keep you waiting."

"Best idea in the history of ever," I say, gasping a little when he removes his fingers.

I swear, everything about Hayes—his attention, his sweet affection, the way he laughs and smiles, just how carefree he is—brings out a side of me I haven't seen in years.

I'm embracing every moment. The fun, the eagerness of fucking, the joy of chasing pleasure.

I reach out and stroke his cock, joining in when he coats himself with lube. The shudder that racks through his body is mesmerizing. Fuck yeah, I did that. Am the reason Hayes's muscles tense, his limbs vibrating.

This man is the ego boost I never dreamed I'd have. Fuck, I'm lucky.

And for the rest of the night, he's mine.

5
PLPG

CHAPTER TWO

HAYES

HEAT WRAPS around my cock as I sink into Sully's ass. "Fuck, you feel amazing," I praise.

His eyes spring open, and he clamps his teeth onto his bottom lip. Like this, flushed, pupils blown, and barely coherent, the man before me is beyond sexy.

I wasn't lying earlier. Wasn't paying lip service to get him to open for me.

The little I know about Sully—the quiet confidence, the flicker of question he can't always keep from his gaze, and the softness of his warm flesh—does it for me. Big time. That, and we've laughed.

Jesus, when's the last time I laughed and had legit fun when hooking up?

It's a bit of a mind fuck.

I grunt as I press fully into him.

A mind fuck, definitely, but fucking into him.... Yeah, he feels perfect.

I drag my hips back, diving into his warmth once again, which earns me a moan. He lifts his hips, meeting me on my next drive into him, and reaches out for me, tugging me down before pressing his lips to mine.

His kisses are demanding, completely at odds with the sliver of uncertainty that I spotted previously. But none of that matters. Not right now.

All I want to focus on are his possessive kisses and the way he feels as I plunge into him.

The next push back in earns me another grunt. We break our kiss, and I peer down at him. I can see the flecks of the hazel in his eyes.

It's intense, being so close to his face, feeling the gentle warmth of his breaths on my skin, but I don't pull away. That's the last thing I want.

His moans grow louder with each thrust, his body arching to meet mine, his hands clutching at my shoulders. Tension builds low in my spine, a coiled spring ready to snap. Each movement, each stroke, brings us closer to the edge, our breaths mingling, our bodies moving seamlessly, as though we've perfected the art of fucking from years of practice, not minutes.

I can barely hold back, the pleasure mounting to an almost unbearable peak. Sully's fingers dig into my skin as he gasps, "Don't stop, please."

"I won't," I promise, my voice rough.

Driven by the need to feel him come around me and see him lose control, I pick up the speed, sweat clinging to my skin and glistening on his as he fucks against me.

"Fuck your hand." I'm too close to the edge and need him there with me.

Inching back so he can get access, I grunt when he wraps his palm around his cock, his whole body constricting and holding my dick in a choke hold. His hand stutters as he bows his back. I cling to his shoulders, focusing on his garbled pleas and the way his muscles tighten around me.

It's all too much.

Too much heat, too much blissful friction—so much so that my hips jerk as my balls tighten and I release inside him with a loud "Fuck" and a deep moan.

I'm still moving, urging him to release, as the first splash of his cum hits my stomach. I groan and lift myself up on my hands so I can see, still balls deep inside him.

Wide-eyed as he watches me, his lips part. I smile before my gaze is glued to his cock and the second spurt that lands on his stomach, dripping into his belly button.

"That's so hot," I say, my voice raspy.

Sully shudders, a final release spilling out of him and dripping over his hand.

He's done. Blissed-out and completely spent.

So am I, but I can't skip out on a taste.

"Give me your hand."

A slow, lazy smirk forms and he aims it my way. He knows exactly what I want from him. I follow his movement as he drags his cum-covered fingers through his release and lifts his hand for me, straight into my open mouth.

I latch on, sucking them clean.

"Jesus." His eyes flare. "Kiss me."

Fuck yes.

After one more suck of his fingers, I release them with a pop before latching my mouth to his and sliding our tongues together as I press my weight on top of him, taking the kiss deeper.

It's slow, but with the tongue fucking going on, I'm practically deep enough to lick inside him and taste my own cum. Humor bubbles inside my chest at the thought.

At my smile, he pulls away. I angle myself so I can see his face and ask, "You doing okay there?"

"I seriously am," he answers, somewhat breathlessly.

Sully searches my gaze. I have nothing to hide. Hell, I know I'm as easy to read as a book. Like a super-simple fourth-grade book. Or so I've been told.

Seeming satisfied with whatever he reads in my expression, he smiles back, fidgets a little, and winces.

"You need me to pull out?" I dance my fingers over his cheekbone. They're defined, not quite chiseled, but set high. Sully really is a handsome guy. And the salt-and-pepper hair is ridiculously attractive. It suits him. Makes him look, I don't know, distinguished or something.

He's not far from a silver fox.

"Reluctantly, yes."

I like his answer. "Agreed. My dick likes being inside you."

He chuckles but cuts it off quickly and cringes. "That may be so, but honestly, it's been a long time since I've... you know...."

I grin. "You're getting shy now?"

He rolls his eyes at me, pink coloring his cheeks, but his smile is big. "Since I got fucked so—"

"Epically. Good and proper. So good, you're going to feel me for days…?"

He clamps his lips together, fighting laughter. I get it, since the last time he laughed, it strangled my cock and made him sore.

It really is time to pull out and clean up.

I do so as carefully as I can. "You okay?" Sitting on my knees between his legs, I peer down at him, trying to get a good read on him.

"So much better than okay."

In that case…. I drop beside him and snuggle up to his side. If he's surprised, he doesn't show it. Instead, Sully turns to face me, still wearing a content smile.

"You want to shower and get a donut?"

"A donut?" His lips twitch.

"I bought some fresh today. Figure we need a sugar kick after expending all that energy so fabulously."

"Fabulously, huh?"

"You know it." I smack a kiss on his lips. I have no issues with post-sex cuddles or chats or sugar sharing. What *is* rare is that I want to with someone I just met.

I hook up as much as I want to, which takes some careful planning with the nature of my work shifts. It also usually means heading out of town. While Collier's Creek has a booming queer community, what it doesn't have is a giant collection of single men who I consider more than a friend.

I haven't had a friends-with-benefits relationship that didn't end in disaster, and since being back in my hometown for five years, the last thing I want is to make things awkward.

But Sully, he's not a local, which is awesome. And if he does stick around…. I let that thought trail off, trying not to examine too closely the flurry of excitement in my chest nor the way my stomach flips over.

We don't know each other. That doesn't mean I'm not interested in getting to know him better.

"You said something about a shower?"

His question tugs me out of my thoughts, and from the loss of his smile, I apparently got a little caught up in my reaction. I do that, though—go on a tangent. At least I kept all my thoughts to myself this time.

"A shower? Absolutely. It's the one room that's

completely finished. It's big enough for two." I bounce my brows up and down like a goober.

"Is that you saying you'd like to join me?"

"I don't have to if—"

"No, I'm happy to share. Water conservation and all that." A fresh glow of pink shines in his cheeks. "It's just—" He clears his throat.

"It's just what?"

"Jesus, I can't believe I'm saying this aloud, and to you of all people."

Confusion slams into me. "Me of all people? Meaning?"

"You know." He gestures in my general direction before continuing, "You. You're what, twenty…?"

"Thirty-one," I answer and arch my brow. A smirk plays on my lips. Obviously Sully's older than me. I've hooked up with a few guys who have had a good ten years on me. Age is just a number, right?

"You're thirty-one?"

"That's what my birth certificate tells me."

His muscles relax a little. "Okay, but still, you're a thirty-one-year-old Adonis."

I wrinkle my nose. "I've heard it, but I have no idea what that really means. Who or what is an Adonis?" I'm not even being obnoxious, which my mom's told me I can be. Just because I've heard the phrase doesn't mean I understand its meaning.

It's so damn easy to miss the point and not read between the lines, so I learned when I was still at school to keep asking questions until someone explained something to me in a way that I understood. I don't give a shit if that's once or fifty times. Nor do I care about anyone's opinions.

He closes his lips as he studies me. I wait, hoping I haven't misread Sully.

If he turns out to be a patronizing—

"Well, Adonis was this guy from Greek mythology," Sully starts, a grin spreading across his face. "He was supposed to be super good-looking, like the ultimate sex god. The kind of guy who could stop traffic just by walking down the street. So, when I say you're an Adonis, I mean you're ridiculously handsome. Like, you're the kind of guy people can't help but notice."

Warmth spreads through my chest, and I chuckle. "So, you're saying I'm mythically good-looking, huh?"

"Exactly." Sully nods, his eyes twinkling. "Basically, if you were walking around ancient Greece, all the gods and goddesses would be like, 'Damn, look at that guy!'"

I laugh outright, the sound filling the room. "Wow, that's quite the compliment."

Sully shrugs, but his smile is genuine. "Just calling it like I see it."

I shake my head, still smiling. "Well, thanks, I guess. I'll try not to let it go to my head." I sober. "Hold on. If I'm an Adonis, what are you? What was with the whole hand gesture?" I mimic how he pointed back and forth between us.

The pink in his cheeks blooms to a bright red. "We can just forget I said anything and agree you're an Adonis."

"Well, we can, but if something's on your mind, I'd prefer to know." I shrug. "I'm a pretty open-minded person."

He studies me in silence before saying, "I can see that."

"So?" I prompt, aiming for gentleness. I don't want to push him and scare him off.

"I'm forty-seven."

I shrug and stare at him. He's hot and we had incredible sex. His age doesn't mean shit to me. It seems like he expects an answer. "Okay?"

"Twice in a whole twenty-four-hour period, let alone a few hours, is not as...." He hesitates. "Feasible as it was when I was your age."

It takes me a few seconds to catch up and figure out what he's telling me. While I hate his embarrassment, I appreciate his honesty. I soften my smile and brush my fingers over his arm. Goose bumps spring up as I trace along his skin. "So you don't think you can get it up again tonight is what you're saying?"

Sully's eyes widen before he snorts out a laugh and drops his head to my chest. His shoulders shake as his chuckles continue.

The sound is contagious. Happy.

Wanting a slice of his sweetness, I wrap my arm around him and shuffle close, dotting a kiss to his head and grinning.

"You've got quite a way with words," he says between his laughter.

"Thanks. It's a gift."

He looks up, beaming at me, gaze searching mine.

"I'm happy to wash you down. Let you do the same. Maybe kiss a little or a lot." In truth, I'd like nothing more.

"Okay."

"Yeah?" My heart stutters in my chest.

"Yeah."

I kiss him before jumping out of bed and heading into the bathroom to turn on the shower. It takes barely any time to heat, thanks to my awesome new hot-water system.

I'm just about to call Sully when he appears in the bathroom, glancing around the recently tiled space.

"You weren't kidding. You've done a great job."

I beam at him. "I can't take all the credit. A few guys at the station helped me. Plus my cousin's a plumber. She's also kinda awesome at tiling, so she spent some time teaching me and the crew how to do it right."

I stop talking, staring expectantly at Sully, wondering why his ass isn't in the shower already. He's naked, still covered in cum. He looks fucking delectable.

I like that his body's not the same as mine. Like it so much, in fact, my dick twinges. But when I can think with my top head enough and peer at his face, I realize something's changed.

"What's wrong?"

He looks like he's sucked a lemon. He swallows deeply before clearing his throat. "Station? Do you work at the sheriff's office?"

I chuckle. "Not a chance Sheriff Morgan could deal with me on a daily basis. He's threatened to arrest me more times than I can count." Shit. That makes it sound like I'm an almost criminal or something. "Not for anything serious. Usually because he thinks I'm a pain in his ass and ask too many questions. Though, there was also the time when I was still in high school and spiked the eggnog at the Christmas Bash. I don't think he quite forgave me for that."

Obviously, I spend a fair amount of time with Sheriff Morgan professionally, but unfortunately on the not-so-pleasant callouts. Those times, I know he sees a very different version of me.

"So, you're a firefighter?"

"Yeah. Became a probie right out of high school."

His shoulders sag, a tight smile forming.

I've heard about this. Sure, a lot of people think firefighters are hot—there's the whole uniform fetish. But some people want to stay far away, sure that firefighters don't make the best dating material.

Since this is a hookup, maybe the beginning of many or maybe this will be the only one, I don't see why my profession should be a problem.

"What's with the frown? You look like someone kicked your puppy. I swear, I think puppies are the cutest."

That gets a hint of a smile from Sully.

I latch on to the win and step away from the shower and into his space.

"You know," I say, tangling my fingers with his and brushing kisses along his neck. I really don't want the night to end just yet. "I've rescued a puppy before, made sure no harm came to its cute head. I wasn't even in uniform."

Sully angles his neck to give me better access, and I internally do a fist pump. At his soft sigh, I smile. When he places his hand on my waist, I want to cheer. Instead, I ease away and slowly walk backward, leading him into the steaming shower.

"Most people think that's adorable."

The spray hits our bodies. I draw him closer, wrapping both of my arms around him.

"Is that right?"

"Uh-huh." I dot a kiss to his lips, and his eyelids flutter closed. "What about you?"

"What, do I think *it's* adorable or *you're* adorable?" He smiles back.

"Either. Both."

A soft sigh passes through his slightly parted lips. "I'm not sure anyone who's adorable could rail me quite as well as you did."

Loud laughter bursts free from me. "Is that right?" I return to kissing his neck while Sully brushes his fingers across the wet skin of my back.

"I think so. It's probably written in a rule book somewhere."

"Probably." I don't stop kissing him, enjoying his soft sighs. It's Sully who squirts shower gel into his palm, making slow work of washing me down until my cock is throbbing.

"When's your next shift?" he asks, working me over with his hand.

My eyes spring open. He's asking me about work now? I'm struggling to remember my own name, so I'm not sure how he expects me to recount my work schedule.

"Huh?"

He chuckles and licks a line up the column of my neck. "Work?"

"Tomorrow morning." Fuck, tomorrow morning. Tonight was definitely unexpected. I have a forty-eight-hour shift to get through starting at seven in the morning. What I should be doing is already sleeping, trying to get rest before my next time off on Sunday morning.

"You need an early night, then." Sully keeps jacking me off, his hand picking up speed.

"Uh-huh." At this point, I'll agree to anything.

"Why not fuck my hand and finally let me know what your cum tastes like?"

"Nngh." My response isn't poetic, but between my fast thrusts, trembling knees, and the jolt zipping up my spine, it's as coherent as I can be. That along with "Fuck!" The word bursts free as I spill into his hand.

Sully's quick to bend and lick at my cock, lapping at my cum before the water can wash it away.

"Fuck," I repeat, this time quieter, as I push against the wall to hold myself up.

As he stands upright, Sully licks his lips, looking completely satisfied. "You need to sleep. It's getting late."

Is it me or did someone turn the shower to cold? "What? No." I hate that he's right. "You can stay, right?"

A soft smile appears as he shakes his head. "I'll head out. That way you'll get a proper rest." He leans into me and peppers a few small kisses on my lips before he backs away.

He can't be serious and be leaving? My eyes drop to his dick. He's rock-hard and just begging for me to taste him.

"Nuh-uh. I'm serious."

"For real?" I pout, which apparently is funny, since his lips twitch.

"For real."

I huff out a resigned sigh, raking my gaze over his wet, naked body before returning it to his face. His right brow is quirked high.

"What?" I shrug. "You look fucking spectacular. Sweet as sugar. From the sip I had, you taste like it too."

With a laugh, he shakes his head, his eyes widening a little. "And you're incorrigible."

Now, I know what that word means. It's been used a fair few times about me.

"Are you going to leave me your number?" I ask. Sure, he doesn't know his plans, but after the short time we spent together, I absolutely want to get to know him better if he does stick around.

His hesitation and lack of response have me frowning.

"Then take mine?" Desperate maybe, but I don't give a shit. Chemistry like this can't be concocted in a test tube.

Sully tugs a towel off the hook and wraps it around himself. He stares at me for a beat before finally speaking. "How about you get through your shift, and we'll see what happens next week?"

What? "So that means you're sticking around and I'll see you?"

"Let's just say maybe." He turns, but before he

leaves the room, he peers back. "Tonight's been…. Hell, Hayes, it's been incredible. Thank you."

And then he's gone.

I hesitate, thinking about chasing him, following him, calling him as he races away, but I stop myself. I like him a lot—more than I probably should after knowing him for just a few hours—but I'm not a sad case who needs to beg for more.

Though, honestly, it's a struggle to keep my feet planted in the shower.

He'll organize an Uber or walk—depending on where he's staying. And despite the glimpses of hesitancy I saw from him, I have no doubt that Sully knows his mind. He's 100 percent a grown-ass man. A ridiculously delectable one at that.

I shove my head under the spray, the ghost of Sully's touch on my cock still lingering.

Looks like I'll wait and see what happens next week.

"Is this a prank?"

It has to be a prank, right?

At my side, Remy snorts. "You can't make this shit up."

Technically, you absolutely could, but… "The callout is really for a cat up a tree?"

For eight years, I've been doing this job in my hometown, Collier's Creek; the five years before that, I was in California, and despite what the movies tell you, a request for firefighters to rescue a damn cat just doesn't happen.

Or it didn't until today.

"Honestly, the details are still a little murky at this point." Amusement trickles loud and clear through every one of Remy's words.

"To be fair, it might be the guy we're officially rescuing," Alice calls out just as she pulls out of the station, engaging the sirens—a little overkill for a cat, but I keep my mouth shut. "Maybe the cat too."

We head down the main street, where a couple of stores are opening. It's barely dawn as we're creeping quickly toward the end of fall, so there are just a few cars that pull out of our way.

"There's a guy?" I'm so confused.

From beside Alice, Captain Zoey Jackson peers over her shoulder at us. "Have you not had enough coffee this morning, Hayes? Try to keep up."

I grin back at her. "There's no such thing as enough coffee, Cap."

True story. It's also why I have zero issues doing

the coffee runs to CC's. Sure, they make the best coffee in town, but as much as I love the crew I work with, not a chance I trust them with the coffee order.

For real. One time Remy came back with a half-strength caramel blend of milky water. And that's not a diss of the baristas—legit, Will, Felix, and especially Cameron make the best coffee ever. Their skills beat any fancy coffee house I visited when I lived in SoCal.

Am I particular about my caffeine? Maybe. Do I also have a sweet tooth to rival Willy Wonka? Absolutely. But when it comes to my coffee, it's not just a drink; it's a masterpiece in a cup (or at least it should be). Okay, so that's probably more of a firm yes to me being particular.

"You've got serious issues, Hayes. I'm going to start looking into a Caffeine Addicts Anonymous group."

I roll my eyes. Cap would not want to deal with me if I went without caffeine, especially when the end of our forty-eight-hour shift is just an hour away.

But back to the cat and man.

"So there's a guy stuck in a tree?" I glance at my watch. "It's barely past 7:00 a.m."

Alice snickers as we turn off the main street and

head to where a few small townhouses are located. We screech on by as I look longingly over my shoulder at CC's. The store light is on, and I can already see a steady morning crowd forming.

"What, is there a time limit for cat and guy tree rescues?" Alice adds.

Not gonna lie, there totally should be.

This morning at the station, I had to rely on our pod machine, and despite the hours I've spent perfecting them, my coffee-making skills just don't cut it. That and we really do need a kick-ass, barista-approved coffee machine.

Cap continues to refuse to add it to our budget requests, but I'm determined to wear her down.

I shrug, releasing a yawn. My adrenaline from the initial reaction to the call crashed pretty epically when I realized it wasn't a life-and-death emergency. Well, as long as this tree climber hangs on, I suppose. I've been sleeping for shit, too, my thoughts constantly replaying my time with Sully. "Maybe there should be. At least until after I've made my first trip to CC's."

"I'll be sure to bring that up at the next town meeting, Hayes. Maybe add it to our Fire Awareness leaflets."

My grin stretches wide, especially as I think Cap

is flipping me off in her head. If I can't start my morning with a good cup of coffee, winding my captain up is the next best thing.

But only because she wouldn't fire me.

I don't think.

Though she's threatened it a few times.

But that's the thing about Collier's Creek and especially family—because, yeah, Cap married my cousin Harriet six years back—you can get away with so much shit, and they love you because of it. Or maybe despite it. I'm never sure which option is the most accurate.

Well, at least in my case, the love is strong. It helps that I'm so lovable—for real. For the last four years in a row, I made the state—yep, *state*—charity firefighters' calendar.

This year I'm December. Arguably the best month.

The competition is fierce, but damn straight I made the cut.

But back to the cat man.

"So the man was trying to rescue the cat?"

"Nah, the other way around."

My eyes widen for a second until I realize Remy is full of shit. I flip him off. "Whatever, man. The guy could have just been randomly climbing a tree, and there just happened to be a cat up there at the same time. Where are we heading?"

"Cottonwood Avenue," Alice answers.

Sweet. My second—completely unofficial—set of parents live there. Abigail, my best friend's mom, should definitely be awake, likely getting ready for work. As soon as the fire truck makes its way down the street, curtains will twitch. However, Alice has turned the siren off. But still, Abigail's bound to hear the commotion, and more importantly, she makes a really good cup of coffee.

Not my favorite kind, but still a decent cup.

She even buys caramel syrup just for me.

Another turn and we're going to hit Cottonwood.

"Hayes, Remy, you guys are on the ladder. Alice, you're with me."

"Got it, Cap," we call out.

We file out as soon as Alice pulls up to the curb.

Huh, we're legit two houses away from Rhys's childhood home. While I don't visit my best friend's folks as often as I should since he moved to New York, this street is as familiar to me as my own.

I glance up at the young cottonwood that's maybe just twenty feet tall. There are barely any yellowing leaves left, most having fluttered to the pavement in the middle of fall. The outline of a man is a dead giveaway of which tree we need to lean the ladder against.

The poor guy. I hope he hasn't been up there long. While the ice isn't too bad, since it only dropped to thirty-six degrees last night, the rising sun that's tipping just over the horizon has dropped the temperature a couple more degrees. It's something science-y I learned when at school, a fact I don't quite understand, but it stuck.

It's unseasonably warm, at least. Hell, today's forecast is a balmy forty-seven. No doubt that means we're going to be blasted with a serious cold snap in the next few days, just to keep us on our toes.

I wouldn't be surprised if we get our first flurry of snow in the next week.

Cap's already next to the tree while Remy and I focus on organizing the ladder.

This street is a quiet one with small-acreage properties, so her words carry easily.

"No shit."

My eyebrows jolt high in surprise, and I peer at Remy. He's staring back at me with the same wide-eyed look.

Cap in public is the consummate professional. *Zoey*, however, has a potty mouth to rival a sailor. It makes sense, since she spent eight years in the Navy.

I have no doubt that's where she picked up all her more entertaining traits.

After Remy unlatches the ladder, we tug it off the rig, sharing another look when Zoey's laughter ripples through the otherwise quiet street.

Who the hell is up there?

I don't hear everything Zoey's saying, but I catch "—paperwork?"

Curiosity has me hurrying Remy forward and calling out, "Where do you want us, Cap?"

She flicks a glance our way over her shoulder, her smile still in place. "Looks like there's a good branch to my right." There's a legit twinkle in her gaze. "You got this?" she asks me.

Hell yes. Not that I'm excited to climb a ladder up a tree, but I love being in the thick of it. *It* being every single thing I can dive headlong into.

"On it, Cap."

With an extra bounce in my step, we reach the tree. I keep my focus on the ladder, making sure not to knock anyone's head off. I have a feeling that *would* get me fired.

Nepotism—a word I learned once Zoey joined the crew—can only curry so many favors, right?

And just to be clear, I was already a member of the firehouse—I moved back home as soon as a rare opening for a full-time position came up eight years ago—before Zoey relocated here and took over as captain seven years ago.

"So," I say, hands on the ladder and angling back, "what have we got—"

Holy shit.

No, like seriously, holy fucking shit.

It's Sully.

Here.

Up a tree.

Holding a ginger cat. Or more specifically, holding Sizzle, the giant tabby belonging to Rhys's folks.

Hazel eyes are locked on mine. They're wide in what I suspect is a mirror image of how wide mine are.

Bright red cheeks don't disguise just how ridiculously handsome Sully is, though.

"Dude." Remy nudges me.

Shit.

"Uh, sorry." I aim for a smile, but it feels weird on my face. What's obvious is that I need to do something, as I completely spaced out. "Sully."

Jesus, his name on my lips…. I swallow hard. Flashes of our night together dance in my brain.

Get it the fuck together, Hayes.

"Soooo." I drag the word out, fortifying myself, determined to keep my shit together. "Come here often?"

Okay, it's bad. I need a Mayday or maybe a flare gun or something to get me out of this situation.

Cap groans, Remy snorts, and Alice, well—I think she's wondering if I'm tripping.

What I need to do is change tack, help Sully and the pain-in-the-ass cat down, and then get myself home and to bed. Maybe Sully could come with me. He's gotta be freezing. I can absolutely warm him up.

"Here's the plan." I aim for friendly and calm as I call up. I've got this. "I'll come up and take Sizzle out of your hands. Then—"

"You know Sizzle?"

My brows dip even as I smile and flick a glance at the damn cat. "Yeah." I chuckle. "Of course I do. I was with Rhys when he got him as a kitten."

Sully's face turns ashen. Worry churns my gut. Fuck, if he goes lightheaded and falls…. I need to get this show on the road and get my ass up the damn tree. Before I can continue, he speaks again.

"You know Rhys?"

My frown deepens. "Rhys Miller?" When he nods, I clarify, "Yeah. He's been my best friend since kindergarten." A flash of horror crosses Sully's features. It's really time to move. "Listen, Sully, let's get you and Sizzle on solid ground. After I have Sizzle, we'll head down the ladder together. I'll be two rungs below you the whole way, okay?"

A little color returns to his skin, and he nods. That's good. Real good. He clears his throat, which I already know is something he does when he's nervous. "Okay. Thanks."

Yeah, he's mortified, which I totally get, but he can barely meet my gaze now. It's bugging me. He said we'd wait until next week. It's only Sunday.

I think I deserve a little eye contact beyond the rush of his "holy shit" expression when he first saw me.

I shake off my frustration. This isn't his fault. Well, being stuck up a tree is his fault. But me being here probably isn't ideal for him, and the gutting truth is, Sully doesn't owe me anything.

CHAPTER THREE

SULLY

IF MY SISTER didn't love this miserable cat so much, I'd have left it up here to fend for itself. I'm sure Sizzle has climbed—and successfully dismounted—this tree a billion times. But apparently, it's this morning, when I had the bright idea to go for a brisk walk before the sun rose, that he chose to escape the house and dart up the damn tree.

The stupid thing still has stitches from a lump extraction. Hence the reason he got stuck and I felt compelled to rescue him.

Look how well that worked out for you.

Maybe if I fell and banged myself up a little—nothing too serious, maybe just some scratches and a sprained ankle—then this cutting awkwardness would disappear.

I peer down at the ground and immediately look forward.

Heights are the worst. It's a really, *really* long way down. And while that's a distraction—albeit a shitty one—from the horror bouncing around in my brain from what I've just learned, I'd prefer not to pass out.

But apparently, I don't need to worry, as Hayes is making his way up, looking frustratingly rugged and handsome—seriously, has he filled out and bulked up since I last saw him?—which is distracting.

Obviously three days won't do that to a man, but Jesus, he seriously does look impressively muscular and sexy in his uniform.

And that is something I absolutely should not be thinking about.

"You doing okay up here?" His voice is deep, carrying gravel that pebbles my skin.

"Yep. Could do with getting my feet on the ground, though." I release a chuckle that is 100 percent awkward and self-deprecating. Middle-aged men shouldn't need to be rescued from trees. It's one of those "no shit, Sherlock" facts that I'm sure everyone knows.

Plus, it's freezing.

I'd managed five thousand steps, which kind of

kicked my ass. The couple of miles was definitely enough to have my legs aching. Honestly, I have no idea how I managed to pull myself up this damn tree.

Being stuck up this stupid tree for what was likely fifteen minutes before Mrs. Mason happened to spot me when she was going to her trash can isn't the best way to start any day. While my perspiration is long gone, I'm seriously cold. Any trace of sweat has, I think, turned to ice.

"We'll have you down before you know it."

I risk a glance at Hayes, and a sigh rushes out of me. He's barely three feet away. Thank Christ.

I latch on to my relief. It chases away my mortification.

"Hey."

That one word and my heart stutters. That he shoots me a lopsided grin, which is exactly as I remember it, doesn't help my reaction to him.

"You ready to hand me Sizzle in a second?"

I nod mutely, not trusting myself to speak. Hayes has paused his climb, his face in line with my stomach.

"Okay. First, let me latch this strap around your waist. That okay?"

As I bob my head, I lift Sizzle carefully, giving Hayes room to work. With deft fingers, he's quick to secure a strap around me. I follow the cord with my gaze and realize he, or someone, has secured it to one of the thick branches.

That I didn't see that happen means it really is time for me to get down and warm.

"Okay, let me take Sizzle from you. When I've got him, I want you to hold on to the ladder with your right hand. Can you do that?"

"Yeah." I flick a glance at the ladder. It's right there, within reaching distance.

"Great. When you've got a good grip, you can move your right foot, place it on the rung, then let go of the branch before holding on to the ladder with both hands. You think you can manage that?"

"As long as I don't look down," I admit.

"You don't need to look down. You just focus on the ladder and don't look at anything lower than my face, okay?"

My gaze connects to his, and I breathe a little easier.

Hayes's steady voice is soothing, carrying a certainty that is less arrogance and more genuine assurance.

While my fear doesn't fully dissolve, his presence alone lets me know he's got this. Got me. And fuck if that doesn't make me sag in relief.

"Okay," I finally answer, not caring too much that it's taken me a while to respond.

His smile is immediate. I lose his gaze when he focuses on Sizzle.

"Come on, Sizzle. I swear you're getting to the end of your nine lives." Hayes reaches out, and I loosen my grip once I know he has a firm hold on my sister's cat. "Jesus H. Christ, no wonder you couldn't get yourself down. I know I shouldn't body shame, but what on earth has Abigail been feeding you?"

A bubble of laughter escapes me. The sound catches Hayes's attention, and we make eye contact. A soft smile forms as he glances up, but rather than cutting it off, I laugh louder, relief probably mingling with hypothermia.

"You doing okay up there?" Zoey calls up. The sound of her voice sobers me pretty quickly.

Laughing my ass off while stuck up a tree probably isn't the safest or wisest move.

"All good," Hayes answers. "We're heading down now."

That's my cue.

With Hayes's heat at my back, we make quick work of descending the ladder safely. As soon as my feet hit concrete, I expel a heavy, shaky breath.

"Let's get you to the rig and checked out." Hayes's warm hand presses against my back.

I feel like sagging in relief, but I'm already mortified. Plus, I realize as I glance around, we've gathered quite an audience.

What I want is to head back to my sister's and evaluate my life choices.

A wave of heat encompasses me as he leads me to the rig, his firm hand doing things to my stomach it has no right to do.

My reaction says everything.

Hayes is under my skin, and I really, really can't have him burrowing his way in further. The ramifications are more than I can process.

"Oh my goodness, are you okay?"

My sister's already at the rig, Sizzle in her arms and worry in her expression.

A wave of warmth washes over me. "Yeah, I am now." I risk a glance at Hayes, who's still rooted at my side, though a frown furrows his brows as he looks at Abigail.

"Shit, you're freezing." Abigail's all frown and concern.

I don't even have the chance to nod and confirm before a thick, warm blanket is wrapped around me. I jolt even as I sigh into the welcome heaviness of the wool. Hayes fills my vision as he stands directly in front of me, tugging the corners of the blanket under my chin.

It's no use. Avoidance is completely impossible.

Flicking my gaze up, I pause and swallow hard when once again, his intense eyes capture mine. There's a slight tilt of his lips, but more than that, curiosity floods his features.

"You know Abigail?" he asks.

Heat hits my cheeks, and I'm fully aware Abigail's still at my side, concern pouring off her while she's still trying to wrangle Sizzle in her arms. "Uhm."

"You probably don't recognize Tom, Michael," my sister says.

Her words snap Hayes's attention to her. "Tom?"

"Yeah, it's been years since he visited here; honestly, you can't have been more than six. Tom's my brother. Rhys's uncle."

I cut my gaze to my sister. A wide smile is directed my way—apparently, she's confident I'm not about to collapse or die of hypothermia anymore. Though, I'm pretty sure I'm dying inside.

I fucked my nephew's best friend.

"Sully?"

At my name spilling from Hayes, I close my eyes.

Abigail chuckles. "Sully? Geez, it's been years since I heard you called that."

Hayes is impossible to ignore, his presence demanding. Our gazes connect and my gut tightens. It shouldn't. If I were a God-fearing man, which I admittedly am not, I'd be worried for my soul and that the lustful thoughts synonymous with *Michael* Hayes would lead me straight to hell.

What have I done?

"I'm…. It's…. I didn't…." I shift under his scrutiny, the blanket slipping a little. I snag it quickly.

"You're also going to be working together at the station. Isn't that incredible?" Abigail butts in, all smiles and clueless of Hayes's scrutiny.

"You are?" His brows shoot up, but there's no accusation in his tone. No, the poor guy looks more confused than a chameleon in a bag of Skittles.

I nod and release a shuddery sigh. I'm still freaking cold, and I'm certain I'm about to have an adrenaline crash. "Yeah. I'm the new office manager taking over from Marge. I officially start in eight days, but I'll be around the station next week to learn the system."

Hayes blinks slowly. A few beats later, he bobs his head. I suspect everything is falling into place—my reaction to him being a firefighter on Thursday specifically.

Fuck knows what his thoughts are about me being Rhys's uncle.

"Isn't that incredible news, Michael?" Abigail pipes up. He immediately looks her way, a warm smile forming. "Are you off tonight?"

"Yes, ma'am. Just about to finish a forty-eight-hour swing as soon as we get back to the station."

Shit. "I'm so sorry," I cut in, mortified.

Hayes shakes his head; this time his smile is all for me. "A callout like this, where everyone ends up safe, is the best way to end a shift."

I suspect he's being generous and that the crew would much rather be ready to clock out, but I appreciate his attempt at not making me feel bad.

"In that case, come over for dinner tonight," Abigail says.

There's an extra heavy thump in my heart, like the bang of a starting pistol, before my pulse races.

"A home-cooked meal at the Miller house?" Hayes nods, a bright smile forming and making his deep brown eyes practically sparkle. "Heck yes, I'll be there."

My heart lurches in my chest. He wants to come for dinner?

Abigail shoots him a pleased smile before returning her attention to me. "Let's get you inside and warmed up."

That sounds like an incredible suggestion. I turn to Hayes, and despite the churning in my gut, I shoot him a smile that I'm sure is all embarrassment. "Thanks so much for… you know, for saving my ass. And the damn cat." I glance around. Most of the crew are packing up, but there are a couple clearly listening in. Zoey's talking to one of Abigail's neighbors. It's Sue, the intake nurse at Collier Creek's hospital. "I really am sorry that you all had to come out here."

Waving me off, Hayes says, "It's all good. It's our job, and I wasn't bullshitting about finishing our long shift this way. It stops the last hour from dragging, so you did me a favor. Hell, I probably owe you a coffee or something in thanks."

Did he…?

"That sounds like a great idea," my sister cuts in.

I flick a wide-eyed stare at her. Her grin is blinding as she peers over at me. The innocence in her expression is far from sweet or real. Jesus, if only she knew that I'd got naked with her kid's best friend. I can't imagine she'd be throwing me in Hayes's path then.

"A good way to end your shift, too, right, Hayes? I absolutely know your first stop is CC's," she says.

Hayes chuckles. "You know it is. No way I can rest until I've had a decent coffee and unwind properly before I crash." He turns his attention to me. "How about you let me buy you that coffee in thirty minutes? I might even throw in breakfast, since you mastered the ladder like a pro." His wink is ridiculously sweet and endearing.

He's also impossible to say no to.

"Okay." It's not gracious, but fuck, that means we have to talk this shit out, right?

"Awesome." Hayes nods and backs away as a couple of his crew get in the fire truck. "It's a date." He bobs his head as I stare wide-eyed at his retreating form.

A date? It can't be a date.

I turn to my sister, more flustered than I care to admit. The woman's smirk is self-satisfied, and her hazel eyes, the shade identical to mine, are lit with amusement. I narrow my eyes at her. "What was that?"

She shrugs and Sizzle squirms in her arms. "I'm freezing my ass off out here. Come on."

She's not the only one. Shit, the blanket. I start to

tug it off my shoulders as I look up when the truck engine starts.

"Don't worry about that. You can give it to Michael tonight," my sister says.

"Hey."

I startle at the sound of a familiar voice and turn, taking in Zoey. "Hey, Zoey. I'm so sorry about all this."

"Puh-lease." Much like Hayes did, she waves it off. "No worries at all. I'll see you Tuesday, right?" She's already backing away as I nod. "Before then, don't let Marge force you to eat a slice of her fruit-cake. Not unless you want an expensive trip to the dentist."

I barely manage an uncertain nod before she jumps on the rig and offers me a wave.

"I forgot you know Zoey." A tug on my arm gets me moving and falling in step with Abigail. "Just one more reason why you made the right call to stick around and take up a position here."

Not committing, I offer a hum. My sister is a force of nature. Her intentions are always good, but she has a tendency to get carried away. Our nine-year age difference sort of gave her a free pass to be the boss of me while I was growing up. Not that she doesn't listen when I say no or tell her to back off.

She does both immediately, recognizing when she oversteps. But the woman does like to interfere.

We step into her house, the warmth making me sigh in relief. I feel frozen to the bone.

"Go grab a hot shower. You have plenty of time before meeting Hayes."

I definitely will, but I need to know… "Don't you think it's odd, me going for a coffee with Hayes?"

This is my nephew's best friend we're talking about. I'm sure to hell my sister's clueless about the effect his offer of buying me coffee and the "date" comment had on me. Why wouldn't she be? But Christ, I'm what, fifteen, sixteen years older than the man. Isn't even the idea of us being friends a bit weird?

"Pfft, Michael's a good kid."

Somehow I hide my wince. *Kid.*

"Wait till you get to know him better. He's such a good guy. Friendly and has time for everyone. We've always adored him."

Her words don't make me feel any better. Especially as the "we" reminds me of how my sister's family feels about Hayes. They treat him as one of their own.

"I'm sure you'll feel the same in no time."

Jesus. If only she knew.

"You've been through a lot, and Hayes is the perfect guy to show you around, help you settle in… help you put yourself out there a bit more," she tags on with an arch of her manicured brow.

By putting myself out there, I'm pretty sure she doesn't mean me being naked and spread eagle in Hayes's bed.

Letting a natural smile settle, I send it her way and nod. It's best I just shower and get this coffee… *meeting* over with.

Hayes didn't appear to be too freaked out. Maybe he'll quickly brush it off with a chuckle and promise to keep what happened between just the two of us. I rub at my chest, ignoring the reason why the possibility of that being his reaction makes me feel worse. I wave Abigail off as I leave the room.

With a sigh, I try to make sure it's my last one. It's no hardship hanging out with Hayes. In truth, I'm grateful, if not a little mortified. I feel like I owe him an apology even though I was as clueless as him.

I'll play it by ear.

As the water sluices over me, heating my frigid bones, I relax. It'll be fine. Hayes is a good guy.

Washing my hair, I consider Abigail's words, continuing to stumble over Hayes being the "perfect guy." It's not even a surprise when my cock chubs.

Hayes's broad shoulders filled out his firefighter's uniform to perfection, and those damn eyes and that smile of his…. I shudder and actively avoid taking myself in hand.

Masturbating over the man who should be—is?—off-limits is wrong. I will my dick to behave.

So why on earth does anticipation bubble in my stomach? *That* and have me picking up the speed as I wash myself down while mulling over which sweater I should wear that will make me look younger than my years?

Wrong.

I wince.

But why the hell did our night together have to feel so right?

CHAPTER FOUR
HAYES

"Your usual?"

My smile comes easily. Not only am I in my favorite store in town, but Cam's cute, in a whole sexy, scruffy, boy-next-door sort of way.

Then, of course, there's the fact that there's been a huge WTF moment in the last hour involving the man I've been getting stiffies over since our hot-as-hell night together.

Like, holy shit! I'm going to be working with him. That means he's not leaving town, which honestly makes my smile grow even wider.

"Maybe, but I'm waiting for someone, so we'll order together. Thanks, Cam. I'm just going to grab a table."

With a smile, Cam nods, his attention swiftly moving to a couple of customers behind me. It's busy this morning. Though it is most mornings I'm here. Rather than the cool temperature encouraging people to stay home, I swear it brings folks out.

At least it's not snowing yet. But according to the radio forecast I heard on the way to CC's, give it a day or two and that'll all change.

I find a seat at the window. It's tucked into the corner a little, which draws me to it.

It'll give us a little privacy to chat. From Sully's reaction, I know it's needed. Because, hello… he's Rhys's uncle. I did not see that coming. At all. As in, color me surprised and put me in a room full of jack-in-the-boxes.

I know for a fact that Rhys's uncle's not been out here for years, or at least not while Rhys still lived here. If he had, I'd know about it and have met him. With Rhys's grandparents living about thirty miles away, his folks tend to head that way a lot for visits. I'm assuming Tom—I scrunch my nose. Nope, he's definitely a Sully. So yeah, I suspect Sully visits them and catches up with his family there.

But back to the holy fuck reveal.

My best friend's uncle. It doesn't matter that

Rhys and I haven't lived in the same town as each other since we left high school—I still count him as one of my two best friends. I worry my bottom lip, not sure how Rhys will react to discovering that not only did I fuck his uncle, but I'm keen to get to know the man.

Not that I'll give Rhys specifics, obviously. Gross for him and talk about awkward.

I look at my phone, my knee bouncing.

It's a weird sensation, balancing my eagerness to see Sully with my nervousness.

Point me in the direction of a burning building or a grassfire, and I'm all over it, no nerves in sight.

Leave me to my thoughts to overthink, and apparently, I turn into a mound of mush.

What if Sully regrets our hot-as-fuck time together?

Concern bubbles through me. Holy shit, what if this is all in my head, and we weren't as good together as I've made up in my memory?

I pause and take a deep breath before rolling my eyes. And not even in my head. Sure, Mrs. Hendricks gives me a strange look, but I'm okay with that. But back to the eye-rolling. Of course bad sex is more likely the reason for his regrets rather than him simply patting me on the head and saying it was fun but can never happen again because of the more pressing issues of work and him being Rhys's uncle.

Shit. I have no clue how I'm supposed to handle this without coming across as needy.

I've never struggled to find a willing partner. But that's not the point.

And fuck, I'm spiraling and out of breath just with my thoughts.

Though seriously, do you know how easy it is to score when you're a young gay firefighter? Not that I'll be sharing that number anytime soon because my momma raised me better than that, and my dad, well, let's just say, he might give me a sneaky high five but then would follow up with a cringe lecture about safe sex and statistics about STIs and oral without a condom.

I shudder at the thought of a repeat of *that* conversation we've had not once but twice.

But back to Sully…. I stand immediately, thoughts cutting off when he enters the coffee shop. He smiles at Cam, and wings take flight in my gut.

My mouth turns dry, he's *that* sexy. His smile lands on the sweet side of coy, making him so ridiculously appealing that I'm instantly reminded why I enjoyed spending time with him.

"Sully."

At the sound of his name, his gaze immediately lands on me, and there it is. That same delicious smile that he aimed my way three nights ago. The problem is the quick widening of his eyes and the drop in the brightness of his smile after a couple of seconds.

Fuck.

"Hayes, hey."

Forcing my worry away, I grin wide, the expression genuine. "You made it." I drink him in. His cheeks are rosy from the cold, and his shoulders seem to lose their tension once properly inside the welcoming warmth of CC's.

When he steps closer, he hesitates, seeming to debate it a second before he reaches out.

I'm not sure if I hide my scrutiny, but I can appreciate this must be awkward for him. Me? Not so much. After the sex we had and the time we spent hanging out, I refuse to let go of the sensation of how he made me feel.

Not second-guessing—despite my move likely being inappropriate as hell—I take his hand willingly, only to tug him close and hug him hard. He lands against my chest with an "*Ooff,*" and he follows up with a chuckle as I pat his back. His coat's cold, his skin freezing.

"I'm so glad you're okay," I say close to his ear before stepping back to take in his features. Beyond all of this morning's reveals, I haven't forgotten the genuine fear when I saw him stuck up that tree. My own or his.

That's nothing to ignore or mock.

"You are okay, right?" Sure, he wasn't harmed, but he was definitely frightened.

The pink touching his cheeks is charming as fuck. It's morphed from the pink only the cold can create to something else. He's making it pretty damn tricky to not swoon hard and immediately invite him back to my place for a morning fuck before I pass out for a few hours.

"Yeah, I am. Thanks to you," he responds, rubbing the back of his head. While Sully's making eye contact, that one move tells me pretty much everything.

He's remembering and feeling super awkward.

I hate that. But what I am is impressed as hell that I can read him.

Assuming I'm reading him right.

Ask Cap and she'll tell you I couldn't read between the lines if it was printed in 500-point font and surrounded by flashing neon lights.

Maybe I should just come right out and talk

about three nights ago. That night, if he'd been able to carry my weight, I would have climbed him like a tree and begged him to stay when he left. But the faint blush sitting high on the apples of his cheeks has me believing bringing it up isn't the right move.

"How about I order us food and drinks, and then we can talk?"

Pancakes that have been obviously soaked in sugar and something hot and frothy in both our guts will make all of this so much better.

I indicate for him to sit with a smile and an up-nod. "My treat, remember."

Seeming relieved to have something to do rather than stand beside me, he nods and starts tugging off his woolen gloves. They look warm and good qual-ity. I know a thing or two about knitting because Cap got me into it a few years back. Something about trying to get me to "sit my ass down before she glued me to the chair."

Weirdly it worked. The whole monotonous task is soothing and captures my attention, and I can usually keep at it for a good hour before I need to have a wander and see what else I can get into.

"That'd be great, thanks." He peers around the coffee shop, and I smile, taking the place in with fresh eyes.

I love this shop, could get legit heart eyes just thinking about it. CC's is pretty much the hub for locals. Not only is the coffee amazing, but I usually come away with gossip and having had at least five different conversations.

Honestly, I'm surprised Francine hasn't already approached me. We've been exchanging knitting patterns for a couple of years now, and last week she told me she'd started work on a sweater for Hank. With Christmas just around the corner, making something similar for Dad would be cool. Though, maybe I should have started on it last Christmas for that to happen.

"What's good here?"

"Pretty much everything. I'm going for a pancake stack. It'll sort me out before I get a few hours of sleep and tide me over until I head out for tonight's feed." Sully finally settles into the comfortable chair, and I check, "Nut allergy, right?"

Immediately, his brows shoot high. "Yeah."

I bob my head and smile, pleased I got that right. Sure, it's only been sixty hours or so, but exhaustion dances in my periphery. Not that I don't remember pretty much everything about our time together.

"I've got you covered. Cam is awesome when it

comes to allergy knowledge and shit. Black coffee, two sugars?"

His eyes widen even further, but I don't have it in me to be embarrassed. So what if I remember pretty much everything about the random shit we discussed? Sully left his mark.

"Err… yeah, thanks, Hayes."

"Great." I shoot him a wink, grinning a little manically as I step toward the counter. "Hey, Cam."

Cam turns from the coffee machine and shoots me a warm smile. "Hey, Hayes. You ready to order?"

I nod. "Sure am."

He steps over to the cash register, dropping a cloth to the side. "What'll it be?"

He's sensible to double-check. Obviously, Cam knows he's one of my favorite people in town because of his kick-ass barista skills, but he also knows I like to occasionally mix it up. Especially with the new holiday drinks on the menu.

"Coffee, no milk or cream for Sully." There's sugar on the table that he'll be able to add himself.

Cameron peers over my shoulder, head angled and assessing. "Is that Abigail's brother?"

For real? Cameron knew Sully's connection to my best friend's family, but I didn't? I definitely need to attend our knitting circle sessions more regularly.

It looks like I've been missing out on gossip. "Sure is."

"I hear he got a new job at the station."

I part my lips, releasing a snort. At some point since I last saw Sully, he accepted the job. That's a given, since he was uncertain about his plans on Thursday. It's only Sunday. I swear, gossip spreads quicker than wildfire in this town. "That's what I heard."

He bobs his head. "That's good for Marge. I know she's been keen to retire for a while now."

He's speaking the truth. Marge is as awesome as she is fierce. She's edging close to seventy and runs our firehouse like a drill sergeant. Sure, technically Cap's in charge, but I'm not convinced any of us really believe that. "She'll finally get to go on that world cruise she's been desperate for." I grin, happy for her.

I'm even happier that Sully's sticking around.

"It's great news. So, one coffee, no cream or milk…," he prompts.

"Let's go for two pancake stacks, and I'd like a caramel macchiato with an extra dollop of whipped cream, some of that caramel powder you have, and a sprinkle of cocoa."

Damn, just the description makes me salivate.

Cameron's lips twitch as he rings up my order. "Long night?"

"Long forty-eight hours."

"Ah, makes sense."

He doesn't even attempt to question my logic of inhaling so much sweet stuff before chasing sleep. I've ordered enough sugary goodness since he's been back in town that he understands my caffeine and sugar addictions.

I pay, and he lets me know the drinks will be brought over soon and that we shouldn't be waiting too long before our breakfast is ready.

With a smile, I turn, lips twitching when I see Sully's no longer alone.

Admittedly, after spending five years in SoCal, coming back to small-town living took a little adjustment. I'm pretty sure I wore the same wide-eyed "what the hell is happening" stare a time or five when accosted by one of the more seasoned locals.

That's the exact look Sully has right now as Mr. DuPont stands next to him, cell phone in hand, apparently showing him photos. Heck, it could be a Facebook exchange or something for all I know.

Photographs of his knitted sailor doll collection is more likely, though.

"Hey." I step to the table and immediately sit

down, facing Sully and appreciating a little too much his pink cheeks and round eyes as they practically beg me to save him.

Do I have a hero complex? Damn straight I do.

Whether it's burning buildings, using the Jaws of Life, or rescuing a gorgeous guy from a tree—along with a pain-in-the-ass cat—I'm here for it.

"Food shouldn't be long," I offer, grinning wide at Mr. DuPont. "How's your morning going, Mr. DuPont? All okay in the world of aliens and secret government bunkers? You know, I heard the lizard people are a problem this time of year."

Mr. DuPont eyes me, not warily necessarily, but more like he knows I'm trying to get rid of him.

Not that he'd be wrong. While Mr. DuPont is a good soul, the last thing I want is for Sully to be dragged into a discussion about whatever conspiracy theories he's currently obsessing over. Not that it can't be fun engaging, but I kinda want Sully to myself.

Before Mr. DuPont has a chance to respond, I say, "You know, the festival is in full-scale planning at the moment. JoBeth said they're looking for extra Santa's elves. I said I'd help them gather recruits. You interested?"

Mr. DuPont narrows his gaze. "You know what I think of the whole festival nonsense."

"Aw, Mr. D., come on, I'm sure I saw you sipping eggnog in the festive tent last year. I'm pretty certain I saw that mistletoe get a workout too."

It's only the latter I'm totally bullshitting about. Mr. DuPont might say he's not a fan of Collier's Creek winter festivities, but I've seen him enjoying at least an element of it every year.

"You know, I think Mr. Henry might be doing the costume fittings."

I'm going to hell. I flick a glance at Sully, who's looking on, bemused.

What he doesn't know is that the word on the street is, Mr. DuPont has been lusting after Mr. Henry for at least twenty years. The same gossip was rife when I was a kid.

Mr. DuPont shuffling his feet captures my attention. I have a moment of guilt when pink touches his cheeks, but the whole elf-costuming thing with Mr. Henry, a man who's been single for as long as I remember, isn't bullshit.

"I'm not sure me getting involved by being dressed as an elf is the best idea."

Huh. That's not a no.

Interesting.

I lose the teasing edge in my tone. "How about you think about it and let me know in a couple of days?"

With that, he bobs his head, tucks his phone away, and hightails it out of CC's.

Watching him leave, I mull our exchange over.

"That was…." Sully trails off, though his voice captures my attention completely.

"Have you met Mr. D. before?"

With a shake of his head, Sully toys with the sugar on the table. "No. I can't say I have."

I grin. "There's a whole town of interesting folks who'll be eager to get the lowdown on you."

"Why does that sound strangely ominous?"

I blink at him. What the fuck does that word mean?

"It sounds like I should be scared."

My smile widens when he clarifies, and there's a gentle flip in my gut over the fact that he didn't make me feel foolish. I study him, taking in his bright eyes. "I'll protect you."

His brows shoot high. "I need protecting?"

"It's kinda my thing." I shrug, not losing the teasing in my tone.

A chuckle spills from Sully. "I'll keep it in mind if

I need rescuing, but I'm pretty sure I can handle myself."

I'm sure he doesn't intend for that to invite my attention, but I can't help it. I dip my gaze lower and take my time letting it roam his body. "I know you can more than take care of yourself." I clamp my mouth shut before I'm tempted to add, "And me." Even though it's absolutely true. He took such good care of me. Twice, in fact.

It's that thought that has me pushing full steam ahead. That and I have zero chill. "I've thought about you a lot."

"Umm." Once again, he rubs at the back of his neck.

"I'm kinda guessing you left because we'll be working at the station together?" I ask.

"You being a firefighter took me by surprise."

"So Abigail doesn't gift you a Wyoming firefighter calendar for Christmas, then?" I ignore his wince at the mention of his sister's name and plow on. "That's good to know. You'll be easy to buy for this year. I'll make sure I get you for Secret Santa at work." If he had received the calendar, I have no doubt he would have had the calendar flipped to February this past year, and March the year before, and then November the year before that all year round.

His brows dip. "What? Should I know what that means?"

I know I shouldn't brag, but... "There's a Wyoming charity firefighter calendar every year." I try to keep my shrug casual, but I'm not sure I manage it very well. Sully's eyebrows shoot high.

"And you're in it?"

"Next year's is the fourth year in a row."

He dips his gaze to my chest, and it's all I can do to stop from puffing it up. I've worked hard to build and keep my strength and fitness. It's a labor of love. Looking good, regardless of how some like to tease, isn't the mission. Being a firefighter is a calling. It's what I was born to do.

The whole six-pack and having people drool over me is just a boost. I'm proud of what I've achieved. My ability to charge into danger and carry people out of burning buildings has saved more people than I can count. And I'll keep doing so as long as I'm able.

I landed a spot in a coveted calendar—well, coveted if you're in the Wyoming Fire Department— and continue to help raise thousands of dollars for homeless shelters and rural locations like Collier's

Creek that rely solely on volunteers. So, damn straight, I'll share my achievements.

"And do you…." He trails off, eyes widening a fraction as pink creeps up his neck.

"Do I what?" When he stays quiet, I smirk, asking, "Have photos?"

He rolls his eyes and huffs out an amused laugh. Less than seventy-two hours ago, we were naked and as up close and personal as two men can get. That he's being coy now, I'm kinda digging.

"Let's get back to me being surprised."

Amusement bubbles in my chest, but not wanting to scare the poor guy away, I nod. "You were surprised, left, but accepted the job anyway?"

"I did."

"Collier's Creek grew on you, huh?" I want to push, tease a little more. Perhaps praise my cock for helping Sully make his decision, but that may be pushing things a little far. Especially as we're sitting in the middle of the coffee house.

There's a steady murmur of conversation around us, and being tucked away a little gives us some semblance of privacy, but it wouldn't take much effort for someone to lean in to listen.

While I like to hear gossip, I don't pass on what I hear too often. Nor do I want it to be about me and

Sully and how amazing it felt being buried inside him. Which is absolutely not what I should be thinking about. Again.

"I think it's awesome you took the job," I add, wanting to pull my thoughts and the conversation back on track.

"Me too. Zoey's great."

I think about the familiar exchange between Sully and Cap over on Cottonwood Avenue this morning.

The scent of coffee growing stronger distracts me, and movement to my side lets me know my caffeine fix is here. I glance up and grin at Cam.

"Damn, that smells so good."

Cam chuckles. "Here you go." He places my coffee before me and does the same for Sully's straight black.

Immediately, I pick up a spoon and dive right in, taking a big mouthful of whipped cream. I sag in happiness, embracing the sugary goodness.

"Cam, you're a genius. Thanks, man."

He snorts. "You haven't even tried the coffee yet."

I scoff and brush away his words. "As if this isn't going to be heaven in a cup."

Sully's light chuckle captures my attention completely. I cast my gaze on him. His smile is bright and real, and I swear he looks a few years younger. Not that he looks old.

And he's not "dad" old. Abigail celebrated her fiftieth birthday maybe eight or so years ago. I don't recall exactly. I just remember Rhys telling me she took a big trip to Europe. The point is, there are a few years between Sully and his sister.

He's still three years away from fifty. And honestly, he's hot and fun and easy to talk to. The sex was in-fucking-credible.

Cam's "Alrighty then, your pancakes won't be long" barely registers. I'm too busy drinking in Sully's smile and thinking about his ass.

I am aware we're left alone again, or as alone as we can be in a bustling coffee shop.

"So, Rhys." I pause, searching his eyes. Most people I'm sure would leave this be, but fuck if I'm not tenacious.

And don't get me started on how I know the meaning of *that* word. All I'll say is, Cap would take credit for it.

As soon as I mention my best friend's name, a flicker of memory slams into me that has my gut churning. Rhys and I talk a couple of times a month, and occasionally, he shares random information about his family. Sometimes even about his Uncle Tom.

The first thing I need to check: "You got engaged or married, right?"

Surprise registers in his expression, but he doggedly stirs his coffee, having put in a spoonful of sugar. He glances away briefly before seeming to straighten out his spine. "Engaged… for a short while."

His tone makes me wince. "I didn't know that part." I twist my lips before admitting, "Honestly, is that something I should be giving you condolences for or saying congrats about getting out before you got married? I never know what to say."

A small smile forms as he makes eye contact, seeming a little more relaxed at hearing my words. "There's no 'sorry' needed, and yeah, I suppose 'congratulations' seems a little… I don't know, bad taste?"

"Well, unless your ex was a fuckface and deserves a nut punch as well as you calling it quits. Then maybe you celebrated hard and had a wild party or something. My friend Shelly did that a few years back when he split from his fiancé. Had a rager and an orgy." Fuck if it hadn't been one hell of a night.

A huff of surprised laughter escapes Sully. "Well,

I didn't have any of that, but I'm kind of wishing I had."

While he's smiling, sadness clings to his tone, and his response? Yeah, his ex no doubt was a fuckface. Not mincing words, I say, "So he *was* an asshole. In that case, you definitely deserve to shed that part of your life."

And I absolutely have just the offer.

Before I can share my brilliant idea, Sully's "I already did" catches my breath. My gaze snaps to his, and I soak up the warmth in his expression and the curve of his small smile.

"Yeah, I suppose you did." And fuck if I'm not happy I was involved in that. I think. Shit, he *is* talking about what happened a few nights ago, right? I usually… okay, *occasionally* keep my ego in check. Before I can blurt my thoughts out, Will appears with our pancakes.

"Here you go. We made sure to add extra cream and syrup on your cherries, Hayes." He places my giant stack that's lashed in so much sugar, I'm sure it would make most people enter some sort of sugar coma. Not me.

"You're the best, Will, thanks." I grin up at him. "Games are starting this week, right?" I ask, referring to the school basketball team that was formed last year by Colton, his other half. The team is young and the kids super green, but I'm sure in a few years, once the kids hit high school, Colton will have one hell of a team on his hands.

"This Friday. Should be fun. You planning on coming?"

"Hell yes. I won't be on shift." I'm also a hardcore basketball fan, both League and college.

"Great." He glances at Sully. "You're Abigail's brother, right?"

"That'd be me."

They shake hands and introduce themselves.

"If you're still in town and like kids fumbling with balls and half-assing their way through a basketball game, the more, the merrier." Will follows up with a laugh.

"Well, with a sales pitch like that, I'll see what I can do." Sully grins.

With a nod, Will says, "Sounds good. I'll leave you fellas to it. Enjoy," before he backs away.

Friday night—we could make it a date. If he wanted. The hot pancakes tempt me to dive on in, but my brain's stuck on possibility… the possibility of hooking up, seeing him more, starting something more serious.

It's not like I'm actively looking for something

permanent—a boyfriend, a husband, a lifelong partnership. But last year, I swear there was something in the water in town. So many new relationships started up.

It kinda gets a guy thinking that maybe having someone to love, to come home to, to care about with their whole heart doesn't sound like the worst way to live.

I take a bite. The sweetness of the pancake is comforting, the buttery, fluffy layers soaking up the syrup in a way that makes each bite just what I need to help get my thoughts together. I focus on the mix of textures and flavors, letting the richness melt on my tongue, hoping to drown out the uncertainty that's lingering in my mind.

I'm more unsettled by the revelations than I've admitted to myself, let alone to Sully. Maybe I should let this go. But I'm struggling to move past our night together. Do I think there's something there? Maybe. The thing is, I'd like to find out and want the chance to get to know him.

I cut my thoughts off with a "Right…," not exactly sure what I plan to say.

"Rhys."

I jump on his words, relieved he's picking up this conversation. I nod. Parting my lips, I pause. I have no idea what to say. How to begin. I contemplate for the barest of seconds before simply going for it.

"We can go to Friday's game together if you want. Maybe go for a couple of beers and food afterward." I pick up my cutlery again, waiting for his expression to settle before cutting into my pancake stack.

"I'm not sure if that's a great idea."

While my gut tightens, I'm not surprised by his response. "Because of Rhys."

"And we're going to work together."

"And you think both are a problem?"

Sully casts his gaze around when the table close by fills up with a couple and a toddler. When he focuses back on me, he says, "Yes."

I shove a forkful of syrup-soaked pancake into my mouth, trying to savor the sweetness and drown out the sourness of rejection. It helps, a little.

I need to change tack. We're both still reeling—of that, I'm sure.

"So, this fresh start in a new town, new job—it all sounds pretty damn awesome. And just in time for the festive season." A sly grin takes over, only a little forced as I try to let go of my lingering disappointment at Sully's reluctance. "There's definitely still openings for Christmas elves."

He snorts out a laugh, and any weird tension dissipates.

This I can do. Make him smile. Slowly win him over.

Talk to Rhys, even.

I'm not sure yet. The only thing I'm certain of is, Sully's got my attention, and I'm sure if I really try, I can talk him into going on a date with me. If that fails, I definitely will be putting the calendar in his Christmas stocking.

CHAPTER FIVE

SULLY

My stomach's full and my cheeks ache from smiling.

"It wasn't that bad." I snicker as I shake my head. We've stumbled into reminiscing about our different times living in SoCal, somewhere I lived before I settled in San Francisco. Not going to lie, discomfort formed like a sticky layer on my skin when Hayes first mentioned Rhys and the reality of our situation, but he cut through any awkwardness with an ease that I'm a little envious of.

"Dude, when you were there, didn't you see the holes in the wall?" Humor lightens his expression. "Don't get me wrong, I've been to a couple of places where that was hot as hell, but that bar was a hovel.

What was the place called again? Something about toads?"

I tug my lips in between my teeth, trying to contain my laughter. This is hardly the place to talk about glory holes.

"In my defense, when I went, I was hungry, new to the city, and I thought it was called Toad in the Hole because it was a British bar."

Hayes's chuckle is loud and infectious. "Holy shit, me too."

Hell, everything about Hayes is infectious, and not in the STI way. It doesn't take much to get caught up in his joy and his easygoing nature. His carefree happiness is all-encompassing.

Simple, almost.

If he's happy, every cell in his body appears to sing, lighting up and shining on the world around him.

Fuck, he's addictive.

"I was with another probie whose parents are British," he says with a snicker. "Our faces when we realized the only sausages on offer did not come with a side of mashed potatoes...." Amusement colors every word as he shakes his head and picks up his coffee. When he does so, a frown appears.

He looks longingly into the empty cup, and my lips twitch.

"You need another? I can ask if they serve their drinks with a side of sausage." My grin is wide. I don't think my stomach can take any more. I've wiped my plate clean and really should already be out of my chair and getting in my steps to try to encourage my metabolism to not give up on me just yet.

Hayes's lips hitch up at my comment, but he shakes his head. "I'd better not." A yawn follows, and I'm reminded he's come off a long shift and has yet to sleep.

"I think that's your cue to head home and to bed."

He sighs and nods, the gesture seeming a little reluctant. "You're probably right."

At his words, we both stand. Hayes turns first, tugging on his coat before he heads out, calling out goodbye to several locals, including Cam, who I've since discovered owns CC's. I follow quickly behind, saying thanks to Cam and Will, the guy who served us food earlier.

The frigid air greets us.

"Still not acclimatized yet?" Hayes grins, his eyes on me, no doubt having spotted my whole-body shudder when the icy fingers of the breeze touched my skin.

"Is it possible to ever acclimatize?"

Hayes chuckles as he takes a couple more steps away from the doorway so people can enter. Quickly putting my gloves on, I follow.

"The first winter after I came home from SoCal sucked. Thought my balls were going to freeze off. But you get used to it. It's kinda awesome having proper seasons, you know?"

Unconvinced, I wrinkle my nose. "I'll take your word for it." I'm half teasing. It's not even snowed yet, though my sister says to expect a heavy fall soon.

Hayes releases another soft chuckle. "After your first winter here, your first Christmas, you'll never want to spend another one without snow or in a place where you can wear a T-shirt in December."

"Uh-huh." I arch my brow, totally calling bullshit. Though, to be fair, the photographs from Abigail over the years she's lived here have been something you'd see on a traditional Christmas card.

While I'm looking forward to a white Christmas —something I've not experienced before—it'll need to be something pretty darn special to have me agreeing with him.

Hayes forms a contagious grin, and not for the

first time this morning, a dimple appears on his right cheek. It should be illegal to be so damn handsome. Add in how sweet and funny and kind he is, it's ridiculously unfair that he has that cute-as-hell dimple too.

"Come on. Let's get you home and warm before your ears drop off and you decide to give up on Collier's Creek early." While he's smirking, he's eyeing my ears as if he's genuinely worried about them. To be fair, they're feeling the cold. "Where are you parked?"

His question pulls me up short. "Oh, I walked."

His brows shoot high before a frown dips them, a small crease then appearing on his forehead. "You walked?" Intense eyes peer back at me.

"Yes?" My confusion lilts my response, making it sound like a question.

My sister's house is only a twenty-five-minute walk away. Twenty if I pick up the pace. And honestly, I need all the exercise I can get. Since I don't do gyms, walking is my go-to.

"Without a hat, a scarf?" Hayes roams his gaze up and down my body as he speaks, and discomfort settles in my chest.

It's been a long time since I've been questioned about what I'm wearing, let alone been under the scrutiny of such a concerned look, which is what I'm sure that is.

"I'm fine," I say pointedly. While I suppose it's kind of sweet—the whole furrowed-brow thing—it's also completely unnecessary. "I'm going to head off, and I'll see you tonight."

He mentioned over breakfast that he was looking forward to dinner at my sister's. Understandable, since she's one hell of a cook.

"Thanks for breakfast," I add, a smile tugging at my lips.

He nods, saying, "I can drive you back. It's no trouble."

My smile settles a little easier. "That's kind, but honestly, the walk will do me good."

I made peace with my expanding waistline several years ago, but that doesn't mean I want to set myself up for a heart attack. Exercise in some form is necessary. Not that I'm going to tell Hayes that.

He may be wearing a sweater, but his exposed forearms when he'd tugged up his sleeves earlier almost had me swallowing my tongue. It was an all-too-real reminder that the man packs a tempting collection of muscles under his clothes.

Pursing his lips, Hayes nods, a reluctant move if ever I saw one. "Okay. I'll see you tonight."

"You will. I hope you manage to get a good sleep," I say before spinning on my heel to head to my sister's.

Hayes saying, "Sully" stops me in my tracks. I turn back, brows high. "Here."

I startle, my head jerking when he steps fully into my space.

"At least wear this," he says as he eases a woolen hat onto my head.

While I'm at a loss regarding his weird reaction to me being hatless, my lips part in surprise as I stand here wordlessly, allowing him to tug the soft wool a little lower so it covers my ears.

His grin is wide, satisfied.

But he's clearly not done, as he removes his scarf.

"Uhm…," I finally manage. "This seems completely unnecessary."

"It's cold and you're going to get ill." Despite his soft voice, there's a firmness evident that makes my stomach tumble.

I work hard at keeping my breathing steady and even as he wraps the purple scarf around my neck. It's warm, immediately fending off the chill from the bite in the breeze. Despite that, goose bumps break free.

It's nothing to do with the frigid air, though, and

everything to do with the ridiculously sweet man. So sweet, in fact, I'm struggling to process his attention.

"There you go. Much better." He tucks the one end away in my coat, a satisfied smirk forming.

"Thank you?" Yeah, I sound as unsure aloud as I do in my head.

"Anytime." He takes a small step back, giving me room to drag in a lungful of biting air. "I'll see you soon. Talk your brother-in-law into making an apple pie if he has time."

My smile comes easily, his comment helping my brain come back online. I don't even wince at the reminder of how he knows Larry. "I'll be sure to pick up the ingredients and leave them somewhere conspicuous. Where he can see them," I add as an afterthought. I'm not even teasing about my intention. Larry is an excellent baker.

Hayes snorts out a chuckle. "Sounds like a plan." He lifts his hand. "Catch you in a little while."

I bob my head, lift my hand, and turn down the street.

I don't look back, despite feeling his gaze on me. Though that could be wishful thinking. I wince. *Wishful?* I try to shake thoughts of Hayes away, especially those locked onto things I shouldn't be contemplating.

The last thing I want is any awkwardness between me and my nephew's childhood best friend. I enjoyed breakfast with him and our conversation. And yes, I'm pointedly ignoring the memory of our night together that's seared into my brain. Breakfast was easy, effortless after the initial awkwardness I felt when I first arrived.

And that's a good thing.

It means we can potentially be friends. I wince. *Friends*. That's all we can be to each other.

Abigail didn't seem to think going for breakfast was a big deal, and while I don't usually give two shits about anyone's opinion of me, my family's opinion matters. The last thing I want is to cause friction.

I head toward the grocery store to pick up ingredients for the apple pie. I'm likely overthinking all of this. As I step inside the store, its bright lights spotlighting the fresh fruit, my shoulders relax a little.

I'm *definitely* spending too much time thinking about Hayes and having more with him. Let's be honest, it's not the first time I've admitted those words to myself. But all through breakfast and the whole him worrying about me thing, it's been hard not to remind myself how easily we clicked.

I expel a shaky breath as I pick out some apples

and place them in a bag. Yeah, I definitely need to stop thinking about what could be and focus on getting my life back on track, starting my new job, and making a go of settling into this community.

Hayes is a distraction I shouldn't be inviting into my world.

AFTER MY INITIAL nervousness about Hayes coming to dinner, the evening ended up being drama free and fun. Hayes stayed on the light side of flirty and didn't make me feel uncomfortable, and the meal was excellent. By the end of the night, I felt more settled—that I'd not only done the right thing with the move, but also that I could find a new home here and friends.

Admittedly the latter isn't up in the air exactly. I have little doubt Hayes and I can be friends. The issue is, he's so damn attractive and easy to spend time with. How can I settle with friendship when such an incredible guy wants to hang out with me?

Which he does. Those were his parting words Sunday night.

They've been bouncing around my brain inter-mittently since Sunday night, not enough to distract me from learning my new role and duties, but enough to get the blood buzzing in my veins, knowing he's already at the firehouse.

It's only day two on the job, and Marge is making the transition effortless—well, I survived my first day, at least. I'm grateful as hell she's sticking around for a couple of weeks. The systems in place work great and are well established. Today, as soon as I get in at nine, she's going to run through the yearly planner—not only the community events, but the booking processes, what professional organizations I need to communicate with, and what additional training and checks I need to oversee.

Knowing Hayes is on-site is already distracting, but the smile that keeps attempting to tug my lips high is a dead giveaway that I'm excited about seeing him as I navigate my car along the busying main street.

I've met the rotation crew—four firefighters who've been welcoming and only hazed me once.

Yesterday, my first day, they had me sit in on a "special meeting" where they presented me with an overly complicated "administrative challenge"—a stack of fake paperwork that required filling out an absurd number of forms, all of which were hilariously outdated or bizarre. There were forms for things like "Unicorn Transport Authorization" and "Dragon Feeding Schedules." I quickly realized it was all in jest when they burst into laughter at my perplexed expression.

After that, they brought out donuts and coffee, instantly making me feel welcome.

The second rotation crew with Hayes on the team started this morning at seven. I just hope I keep my shit together and don't get all flustered.

Shit.

What if he's told someone about our hookup?

The thought almost stops me from putting my blinker on to instead drive past the entrance to the station parking lot. With a nervous dip in my stomach, I sigh and pull in.

If Hayes has, then so be it. There's nothing I can do about it after the fact. We never discussed how we were going to handle everything. Plus, it's not like I haven't told my friend Austin. It's not something I would have usually called him up to share with—maybe when we were in our twenties, but not now in our forties.

But on Sunday, once I realized who Hayes was, damn straight I called him up with my "holy shit" moment.

The asshole had laughed, thought the damn thing

hilarious, had even put me on speakerphone. I've only met his partner, Jasper, a couple of times over the years, and honestly, I think I might dump Austin as my close friend and swap him for his boyfriend. Jasper was a lot more sympathetic than my old college friend was.

Zoey's outside talking to…. I study the Black man at her side. Remy. With so few firefighters on rotation, I made it my mission to examine the framed photographs on the wall yesterday. Usually, I work with a lot more people than this, so I made sure I committed the names and faces to memory yesterday.

There's a team of volunteer firefighters on call should extra support be needed. I'm determined to learn all their names and faces, too, by the end of the week. Living in a small town like this, it's good to know who's who.

"Hey, Sully," Zoey says. Rather than offering me her hand, she hugs me in greeting. She was only around briefly yesterday, since it was officially her day off, but she made it crystal clear that the Collier's Creek station is very much a family. She also latched on to "Sully" rather than my given name; I suspect she overheard Hayes last week.

"Hey, Cap." My lips twitch as I pull away.

She rolls her eyes but doesn't call me out for using her moniker. "Remy." She indicates the man at her side. He's about the same height as Zoey, with wide shoulders and startling eyes. "This is Sully. Marge is making sure he knows the bullshit you all try to pull so he'll be prepared for anything."

Remy's smile is wide when he shakes my hand. "Don't listen to Cap. She's just pissed Hayes won't buy her a cinnamon swirl from CC's. Harriet's given him strict instructions."

I quirk my brow and smirk at Zoey. I don't know Harriet beyond that she's married to Cap.

Zoey just rolls her eyes. "Let's head inside. Hayes will be back any minute from the coffee run," she says, and I struggle to ignore the way my stomach somersaults and my pulse flutters. "I'll introduce you properly to the guys. Then, this morning, I'd like you to shadow one of the crew, just to understand the day-to-day runnings."

"I'll be what now?" For years, ever since finishing college, I've sat my ass behind a desk.

Zoey chuckles lightly and pats my shoulder. "Nothing to worry about. You can get back to the safety of working with Marge on the schedule this afternoon. It's important to have at least a semblance of understanding of what we do here, what's expected of our firefighters. That way, when you're trying to do your job, you'll be able to navigate your way around the team and balance expectations versus reality better."

As she speaks, my brows rise higher and higher. They're so close to touching my hairline, there's no doubt her "nothing to worry about" response missed its mark.

Zoey indicates for me to follow her while Remy gives me a friendly shoulder nudge. "Don't sweat it. We're not *that* bad."

"Hmm." I give him a side glance. I kinda read through the lines that getting the team to do anything—complete requests, fill in paperwork—is going to be like wrangling cats. It can't be that bad, right? It's not like Zoey won't run a tight ship. The tour yesterday told me a lot—everything was clean, well maintained, and organized, not only the station itself, but most definitely the administrative side of things.

"I think she just wants you to know that while things can be super chill here, they can also be a bit manic. So if, for example, we're up all night on a call, and you rock into the office when we've just gone to bed to try to get a couple hours of sleep, that won't be the best time to ask us to do anything."

I nod. "That makes sense." It would just take some adjustment, working in an environment where I'd be left to my own devices a lot of the time while trying to organize things with a team whose day would not necessarily ever be the same.

We head into the communal room. The space is quiet, much like it was yesterday. But with only four full-time firefighters on duty at any given time, I've been told this is the norm. I've also been told that when the fifteen volunteers come in for training, the station's a much busier, more hectic place.

"Listen up," Zoey says as she directs Alice and Remy to the large table that's big enough to sit twelve. "Tom Sullivan, Sully, will be replacing Marge in a little less than a couple of weeks. It's not your job to scare him off and have him questioning his life choices."

The pair before me grin, and with their eyes already on me, they nod in my direction.

It takes less than two seconds for Remy to ask, "Are you the cat guy?"

Expecting this, I chuckle and rub the back of my neck. "Guilty as charged. What better way to figure out if I'd fit in with a firehouse team than by meeting you all on a callout?" I'm full of shit, but the snickers around the table are on the right side of teasing rather than ridicule.

"Sully here is also Abigail's brother," Zoey adds.

Alice's eyebrows shoot high. "No shit." She casts a glance behind me. A sprinkle of awareness has me catching my breath and straightening my shoulders. Alice continues, "Isn't that your boy Rhys's mom?"

As much as I'd like to not look at Hayes, my gaze naturally gravitates to his as he reaches my side, two coffee trays in his hands. His gaze meets mine, his smile quick to form. At his proximity, my muscles loosen rather than tightening further.

"One and the same."

"So you know each other?"

"No," I'm quick to say.

Hayes arches his brow, a question forming in his eyes. He then glances at Alice. "Not really. I think I may have met Sully once as a kid. Not enough to recognize him."

I slowly expel my held breath. Hayes hasn't told anyone about last week. This time when Hayes looks my way, I offer him a small smile, grateful he's kept this to himself.

"Sully and I go way back," Zoey says. "It was a complete surprise him being here, though."

"I swear," Remy starts with a snicker, "if you all

say you're related, second or third cousins or some shit, I'm going to buy you banjoes for Christmas."

As Zoey shakes her head, I grin, my shoulders fully relaxing.

"What do you expect from small-town living?" Alice shrugs. "If someone's not related or doesn't know a friend of a friend's dog, then you're never going to settle in or be prepared for a place like Collier's Creek."

"Were you born here?" I aim the question at Remy and Alice, since I know Hayes was, while Zoey is a transplant like me.

"They wish they were that cool." Hayes shoots me a wink. On cue, butterflies take flight in my stomach. I swear, the man only needs to breathe in my direction and he pulls some sort of reaction from me.

I'm grateful this time it's not my dick saluting him.

Alice answers first. "My dad was born here but moved away for college and never headed back. I was brought up in Tennessee." When my eyes widen, she chuckles. "College numbed my accent a little. Teaching a little bit more."

"You were a teacher?" I ask.

"For a year before I realized it wasn't for me. It didn't take me long to figure out firefighting was. I headed this way a few years back. Moved in with my grandparents."

Damn, she wasn't lying about the family connections. I turn my attention to Remy, wondering what his connection is to Collier's.

"I just moved here nine months ago."

"Really?" I ask.

"Yeah."

When he doesn't continue, Hayes throws a balled-up napkin at him. "Don't be a dick. Tell Sully your connection."

From the way Hayes is grinning, I wonder if this is the friend of a dog's friend connection.

"My cousin's friend moved here last year."

I wait for more. When it doesn't come, I force my furrowed brow to smooth out. "Okay. So he's your friend too?"

"Not then, no."

"Jesus, Remy. You're making it sound like you were running from the mafia or something." Hayes throws another balled-up napkin at Remy, who ducks it with ease.

"How did you link anything I just said to the mafia?" Remy snorts in amusement.

Completely ignoring Remy, Hayes says, "His cousin's Cassius Britton."

What? My brows shoot high, and I openly stare at Remy. If he's bothered by Hayes's oversharing, he doesn't show it. Instead, he shakes his head and rolls his eyes.

"*The* Cassius Britton?" The question fires out of me. "As in, the Minnesota Eagles player?" *Holy shit.*

"That's the one. And don't get too excited. He's nowhere near as awesome as I am." Remy chuckles.

Alice snorts. "Uh-huh. Professional basketball player or firefighter in Collier's Creek…. A toss-up for who made the best career choice."

"Cass only wishes he could make it as a badass firefighter," Remy fires back, throwing me a wink.

"I'm sure." I smirk, trying to process the connection. "So, his friend?" I ask curiously.

"You remember Will from CC's?" Hayes says. He's been quietly passing around the coffees before turning to look at me, handing me a to-go coffee cup. When I nod, he says, "His partner, Colton, almost made it to the League. Met Cass at that elite basketball college camp they have every year."

"No shit?" Every basketball fan knows about Montview. It produced some impressive players over the years, Cassius Britton being just one of them.

"Yeah, he's the head coach of the kid's basketball team Will was talking about."

Just as I'm about to nod, Remy interrupts, saying, "Y'all went to CC's?" It's less of an accusation, more of a confused "I thought you said you didn't know each other?"

I still. Maybe blanch a little.

I don't have a chance to respond—thank Christ, since I have no idea what to say—as Hayes answers, "Yup. Also had a slice of Larry's apple pie Sunday night too."

"Shit, man, and you didn't get us any?" Remy complains.

"It needs to be eaten fresh to really appreciate it," Hayes responds, a grin forming as he settles in a chair at the table. I'm relieved he shifted the conversation away, shining the spotlight on his connection to me being that of a family friend.

I sip my drink, appreciating yet again what good coffee they serve at CC's, and even more than that, how Hayes remembered my order for the second time. He's incredibly thoughtful. I inhale the scent of roasted beans and smirk when the group keeps firing fun digs at each other before Zoey reins them in.

A gut-deep rightness settles inside me. There are

no assholes on the team. No one here who I think will try to backstab me. And the man at my side inhaling a coffee that smells so sweet, I think it would make even a bee fall into a sugar coma, well, with the way he deflected and took the heat off us, I'm sure he's more than just a pretty face, a pack of lickable abs, and an incredible fuck.

Not even half an hour of being on the job with him and I've got a feeling that Hayes has an arsenal of ways he's going to get under my skin and make it impossible to simply keep things professional.

5
F L C

CHAPTER SIX

HAYES

I'VE SPENT the last few hours with Sully attached to my hip. Unfortunately not literally, but it's still been fun showing him the ropes and the sorts of things we spend our day doing when not on callouts.

When we hooked up, our age difference didn't really register on my radar. Now, though, I don't know. It's a little more obvious—and sexy as hell—in the way he carries himself. He's calm, confident, and sharp as a tack. He's just a little shorter than me, but he's got this presence that makes it seem like he's the one leading the way. Every question he asks is direct and to the point, like he's already thinking three steps ahead. It's clear he's efficient, but I can't help noticing how that professional exterior of his softens just a bit whenever we're alone.

I like it a lot and have become progressively needier for his attention as our time together keeps trickling on by.

We started the day with some basic chores—nothing too glamorous but crucial nonetheless. First up was gear inspection. I showed him how we clean and maintain everything from the hoses to the oxygen tanks. He listened intently, asking all the right questions, but there was something about the way he did it that made me wonder what he was thinking beneath that composed demeanor. I took every opportunity to brush close as I demonstrated something, keeping my tone light and playful though subtle enough that the others wouldn't notice.

That's the last thing I want—or more specifically, I don't think *he* wants anyone to know what happened between us. And I get it. I really do. Sure, I can be dense at times, but my mom always told me you have one chance at a first impression.

I want him to fit in here. Be happy in Collier's Creek as well as the firehouse.

After chores, we head over to the kitchen. Cap is chopping vegetables for lunch while talking through her headset to whoever is on the other end of the call. She gives us an up-nod and mouths, "I'll be a while," so I figure it's a good time to show Sully the communal side of life here.

"We all take turns with the cooking and cleaning," I explain, grabbing a sponge to start wiping down the counters. I catch his eye and give him a small, teasing smile. "Can't let you off the hook, Sully. Everyone pitches in."

He chuckles, a deep sound that sends a shiver down my spine, and takes the towel I hand him. His fingers brush mine, just for a moment, but it's enough to send my thoughts skittering. I keep my focus on the task at hand, but I can't resist a few more stolen glances his way.

As we finish up in the kitchen, the sound of laughter filters in from outside. The other two members of the crew are shooting hoops out the back where we have a small courtyard.

"You play?" I ask Sully, nodding toward the door.

Remy and Alice can't have been out here long. They're still wearing their thick sweaters, not having warmed up enough to peel off the layers.

"I haven't in years," he replies with a smile, one that crinkles the corners of his eyes.

"Well, no time like the present," I say, bumping his shoulder lightly with mine. Before we step outside, I tug a spare hoodie emblazoned with

Collier's Creek Fire Department off a hook and pass it to him.

He shifts awkwardly, lowering his voice as he says, "You've got a thing for the cold?"

I grin, immediately amused. "Not really. More like I've got a problem with *you* getting your cute ass frozen by not being warm enough."

I don't wait around for an answer, already knowing I've probably said too much, considering where we are. As we step outside, I focus on basketball and Sully telling me he hasn't played in a while. "It's good for team morale," I say, explaining why we hang out in the courtyard even when it's cold enough to freeze our nuts or tits off. "Plus, despite who Remy's cousin is," I add, pitching my voice high so my friend can hear me, "Remy can't play for shit. You'll make him feel better about himself with a couple of games of two-on-two."

I ignore Remy cussing and flipping me off and shoot Sully a smirk instead. He's staring at me with an arched brow and an amused expression.

"You sure you want me out there?"

"Absolutely," I say, angling fully away from Alice and Remy and lowering my voice just enough so only he can hear. "Plus, I wouldn't mind seeing you in action."

That earns me two raised eyebrows and a faint smile, and I can tell he's tempted. Finally, he steps onto the makeshift court, and it's not long before he's joining in, a little rusty but clearly enjoying himself. I can't help but watch him, impressed by the way he holds his own.

As the game winds down, I sidle up next to him, leaning in close enough that only he can hear. "Not bad, Sully. Didn't think you had it in you."

He gives me a sideways glance, his eyes twinkling with something that looks like amusement. "There's a lot you don't know about me," he says, his tone light but layered with meaning.

I grin, letting the moment hang in the air between us. "I look forward to finding out."

For now, though, he has paperwork to get back to, so I'm going to have to let him go. But I'm already looking forward to the next time we're alone and the chance to peel back another layer of that cool, efficient exterior.

"Come on. I'll walk y—"

The blare of the alarm pierces the air. Our gazes connect, and my grin is quick to form while he becomes wide-eyed, and I can't tell if he's panicked or excited. Maybe a little of both.

"Let's go." I move immediately, heading for my cubby.

Sully, hot on my tail, calls, "Me? You want me to come out with you?"

I flick him a glance. "Sure do." That's all I offer while I suit up, the crew around me doing the same thing.

"Alice," Cap says, already standing next to the rig in her gear, "we're heading to Sallinger Crescent, off Broadbank. Chimney fire."

A throb of excitement pulses through me. All I hope is that the fire's contained and no one's been hurt.

"On it, Cap." Alice is all efficiency when she jumps in the rig, starts the engine, and slams her door closed. That's our cue to get moving.

Cap nods when I usher a still wide-eyed Sully into the cab. Sure, no one really wants to deal with a fire—or that's our official line—but that Sully's here to witness it makes him weirdly lucky. That seems like a crazy-as-shit word to use, but this time of year, our main callouts tend to be vehicle collisions. Those can be brutal. A fire, though, especially a chimney fire, is usually quick to contain and rarely has casualties.

We're buckled in and tearing out of the station as

Cap gives us a breakdown. "It's a small residential fire, likely just the chimney. Should be contained if we get there in time, and we're only three minutes out. I've got a couple of volunteers on standby, but I don't expect we'll need them. Let's keep it tight, keep it safe, and get it out fast."

I glance at Sully, catching the sheen of nervous excitement in his eyes, which is sexy as hell. He's also going to see me in action, and I kinda love that.

We pull up to Sallinger Crescent, and the first thing I notice is the smoke—thin, gray wisps curling out of the chimney, not yet thick or black, but enough to set my pulse racing. This is what I live for. The anticipation, the surge of adrenaline that hits the second the rig comes to a halt. I'm out of the cab before it's fully stopped, the world narrowing down to a sharp focus as I take in the scene.

The house is small, single story, with a cozy feel that clashes with the urgency of the situation. The scent of burning wood lingers in the air, mingling with the crisp bite of the cold. My breath fogs as I exhale, heart pounding, but it's not fear that drives the heavy thud—it's the thrill, the deep-seated knowledge that I was born to do this.

Cap's out of the rig next, assessing the situation with a practiced eye. "Hayes, you and I will take the roof. Remy, get the hose and be ready to hit it from the ground. We keep it contained to the chimney. Make sure no embers spread. Alice, check everyone's out and safe."

"On it," I reply, as does the crew, already moving into action. There's no hesitation, no second-guessing. My body knows what to do, my mind already mapping out the steps. Suit up. Check the gear. Breathe. I've done this a hundred times, but every callout still sends that electric jolt through my veins, a reminder that this job is never routine.

"Sully, stay by the truck," I say as I grab my gear, my tone firm but with a hint of the playful edge I've been using on him all day. His wide-eyed look shifts into something more resolute, and he gives me a short nod. "We've got this," I add, the words laced with the confidence that I know he needs to hear right now.

Cap and I collect the tools we need—axes, pike poles, and the roof ladder—and head to the side of the house. We work in sync, every movement delib-erate. During our ascent, heat pushes against us as it rises from the chimney, the crackle of fire just barely audible over the pounding in my chest.

We reach the roof just as the deputy's car arrives on the scene. I spare a glance, relieved to see it's

Dakota. He may be new to the position, but he's steady and efficient in a crisis. I turn my attention back to the task and steady my breathing. The smoke is thicker here, swirling around us like a living thing. It's not just the physical challenge of the job that gets me going; it's the intensity, the controlled chaos that makes every second count. This is where I'm meant to be, right in the thick of it, balancing on the edge between danger and control.

Cap works swiftly beside me, her focus razor-sharp. Together, we assess the chimney, spotting where the fire is hottest. The flames are confined for now, but it won't take much for embers to spread to the roof if we're not fast. I move quickly, but every action is calculated, each step deliberate. There's no room for error up here.

"Got a good angle," Cap says, and I nod, positioning myself to get the pike pole into the chimney. We need to break up any blockages, clear the way so the fire can be extinguished fully from below. Remy's on the ground, ready with the hose. We're a well-oiled machine, each of us playing our part in a dance we've rehearsed a thousand times.

"Remy, hit it now!" I call into the two-way attached to my jacket, and as the water rushes up through the chimney, the fire hisses and sputters, fighting its last battle. I can feel the rush of steam against my face, the sharp contrast of heat and cold, and it makes my blood sing. This is the part of the job I'm addicted to. The moment when you stand at the brink of disaster and pull it back from the edge.

As the fire diminishes, I take a moment to glance down at Sully. He's by the truck, but he's not just hanging around—he's talking to Dakota and the homeowner, an older woman, someone I vaguely recognize, who looks like she's been through the wringer. She's standing there in slippered feet, clutching her coat tight around her, her eyes wide with worry, but Sully's calm, steady presence seems to be helping. He offers a good balance to the more serious deputy at his side.

Sully pats the woman's arm while nodding at something Dakota says. Sully getting involved isn't what he was asked to do, but it's exactly what she needs. Watching him like this, I feel a different kind of heat rise in me.

With the fire out, Cap signals for us to wrap it up before she heads over to Dakota. We lower the ladder, pack away the gear, and head back down to solid ground. My heart's still racing, but it's a good feeling—one of accomplishment, of a job well-done. I glance over at Sully, who's now gently reassuring the homeowner that everything's going to be okay. He meets my eyes, and there's a look there, something deeper than just excitement. Maybe it's respect. Maybe it's more.

"You did good," I say a little while later as we climb back into the cab, my voice low and edged with something only for him.

"So did you," he replies, that faint smile back on his lips.

We buckle in, ready to head back to the station, but the energy between us has shifted. It's charged with the exact same something when we first met, something I'm eager to explore. As the rig pulls away, the thrill of the fire still thrumming through my veins, I shift my thigh, deliberately pressing it against his.

He has plenty of room to move, to pull away, but he doesn't.

I don't hold back my smile, but I make sure I don't direct it at him. Instead, I peer out the window, watching the familiar streets and houses I grew up around. I love this town and its people. That Sully's found his way here has to be more than a happy coincidence, right?

Okay, so yes, his sister lives here, but the spark between us is as hot as those flames we just doused.

With a gentle breeze and a little kindling, maybe we can keep it burning bright.

Cap's "You doing okay, Sully?" snaps my attention back to the cab and my crew. She's eyeing Sully, who straightens a little under her attention.

"Yeah. It was all a little intense."

Cap bobs her head. "It always is." She shoots him a grin. "Hell of a second day, huh?"

At my side, his thigh still against mine, Sully chuckles. "You can say that again. An eye-opener for sure." He glances around at the four of us. "You all just sort of moved as one, seemed to know what one another were thinking." He shakes his head, and I'd like to think it's awe I hear in his tone.

"That's a hell of a scary thought," Alice calls out over the sound of the engine. "There's usually only a couple of things on Hayes's mind."

A chorus of "sugar and coffee" follows from all three asshole members of my crew.

Sully chuckles, and I drop my gaze to his lips before meeting his eyes. "Don't listen to a word of it."

He quirks his brow. "Are you saying you don't spend a lot of time thinking about a caramel macchiato with an extra dollop of whipped cream?"

Out the corner of my eye, I see Cap staring at the two of us. Rather than making it clear that since our night together, Sully is taking up a lot of real estate in my mind, I force my tone to pitch toward teasing when I say, "Well, I'm not going to say I don't think about a *caramel macchiato*, but let's just say there's another blend that's been keeping me up at night."

From the way he shifts and ducks his head, it's clear I'm being as subtle as the sirens on our rig. In my defense, reining in the need to flirt with him and pull a reaction from Sully is practically impossible.

Thankfully, there's no time for him or anyone to respond as we pull into the station. My focus turns to straightening out my gear, cleaning the rig, and preparing for the next callout. It doesn't mean I don't watch Sully leave with Cap at his side.

Nor does it mean I don't catch his final subtle glance my way before he disappears around the corner. I swear, watching the man walk away is like trying to look away from a fire—it's almost impossible, and I'm left feeling the heat long after he's gone.

CHAPTER SEVEN
SULLY

"Where'd you get the hat and scarf?"

I stop in my tracks and peer over at my sister, who's already holding a glass of wine and has been buried in her Kindle for an hour.

Touching the soft wool on my head, I offer, "Hayes." I try for nonchalance, but I'm not sure Abigail's buying it. While there's a decent age gap between us, so it's not like we hung out lots as kids—hell, when I was a tween, she'd almost finished college—she still knows my tells.

She quirks her brow high and takes a sip of her drink, pinning me with her stare.

What I should do is wave her off and get my ass out of here. I'm heading to the basketball game, then out for drinks after with Cap's crew. They overheard

Hayes talking to me about Friday's game and swiftly invited themselves along. Apparently, there's not all that much to do in town—especially weekly beyond high school football or the occasional band playing at one of the bars—so the introduction of basketball has been supported enthusiastically by locals.

"What?" I roll my eyes at myself. I swear, big sisters, even when in their fifties, have the power to manipulate from a stare alone. It's impressive really, but I'm not a fan of it being directed my way.

"It looks like one he knitted himself."

Knitted himself? "Hayes knits?" That's not something he's shared with me. Instinctively, I touch the scarf that I tried once—halfheartedly—to return to Hayes, but with a smile, he insisted I keep it and the hat.

"Yeah. He's pretty good too. He's in the knitting circle. Managed to get a few guys and younger folk to join. Apparently, knitting is what all the cool kids are getting into these days. It's 'lit' or whatever."

I snort. "Lit, huh?"

Abigail pulls a face at me. I'm tempted to tug out my cell to take a photo. I can't imagine the kids at her school would believe this was the way their assistant principal behaved.

"So, who did you say's going out for the game and drinks tonight?"

I press my lips together. "Are you missing Rhys or something? Feel like going into mom mode?"

"Fair point." She places her wineglass on the table. "It's good you're heading out, making friends." Her tone softens. Abigail knows full well the shit-show of my ex and the oftentimes toxic environments of my working life.

I won't get into any crappy emotions, though. Not now when I'm embarrassingly keen to go and watch kids chasing a ball around a court. Admittedly, my eagerness has a lot to do with seeing Hayes outside of work. That we've got chaperones is probably a good thing.

I snort out another chuckle. "Thanks, *Mom.*"

"Oh, fuck off. You know what I mean."

Her cussing has me laughing harder. "I do," I say when I rein myself back in. "Everyone at work, both crews, are great. I'm enjoying being in such a different environment and out of corporate."

"I can tell." She angles her head, studying me intently. "And the hat and scarf look good on you."

I ignore the tease in her voice, unwilling to read more into it. With no idea how she'll respond if she discovers my involvement with her son's best friend, I have no desire to spend more energy on it.

Not yet. Maybe not ever. Though considering my eagerness to see Hayes, I suspect the time might come soon enough. I'll just cross that bridge when I come to it.

With a "Thanks," I wave goodbye and head on out. I'd only come into the main house to sort my laundry, but it's a reminder that if things do work out at the fire station, I should look for a more permanent place to live in the New Year.

Collier's Creek is beginning to feel a lot like home.

The biting air snaps across my exposed cheeks as soon as I step outside. This morning there was a light flurry of snow, but it stopped around midday. Even if it does pick up again later, it seems a lot more sensible for me to walk to the high school where the basketball game is.

I have zero experience driving in the snow. So, me behind the wheel would be dangerous to the town's residents. One day soon, I'll have to bite the bullet and take a chance, but today's not the day.

It's already dark, but the streetlights illuminate the way, so I can easily see the pavement that'll lead me in the right direction. I step onto the sidewalk from my sister's drive and come to an abrupt stop at the sound of a car door closing.

Hayes rounds the hood of his truck, a grin stretched wide, his eyes bright. Fuck, he's handsome.

He's also here.

"I suspected you'd walk."

His words startle my brain into working, and an easy smile slides into place.

He's here for me. The thought has my insides going all gooey, which isn't as unpleasant as it sounds.

"You did, huh?"

"Yep." He nods as he approaches me, his gaze moving to my hat before dipping to my neck and the warm scarf. I flush, despite him already having seen me wearing both earlier this week. "Thought we could make the trip together."

Heat floods my chest. How a guy as hot as he is ended up so sweet is difficult to comprehend. While I hate stereotypes as a rule, I have years of firsthand experience that makes the man before me a unicorn.

A shiny, ripped-abbed, firefighting unicorn.

"That's mighty chivalrous of you." I step closer to the car. Sure, it's really Hayes I'm edging toward, but I feel the need to pretend a little longer that we can make it as "just" friends.

Do I want more? I think I do. But I need to be

sure. Diving in headfirst with a man with such strong ties to my family could end up being a nightmare. Being certain is smart. But every cell in my body is protesting that there's still too much space between us.

"My dad taught me right." He follows up with a wink before turning and opening the passenger door for me. His arched brow and sweet smirk comes with a silent "See?" And I absolutely do see. I also think his dad is a smart man and deserves a reward or something.

I say as much to Hayes as I settle into his old truck, my muscles relaxing when the warmth in the old cab wraps around me.

"I'll be sure to tell him." He grins as he starts the engine.

"You get on well with your folks?" I ask. I'm curious about the people who raised him. What will they think if we start dating? An age gap is one thing that I know some people get worked up about. Add in my connection to Rhys, and that's got to cause some sort of reaction, right?

"I do." He pulls away from the curb. "They divorced when I was thirteen and seemed to do it all as admirably as possible, you know?"

I blink. *Admirably?* I nod while saying, "Even if

amicable"—I deliberately don't put stress on the word, but I don't ever want him to be in a situation when some asshole might mock him for using the wrong word—"it still must have sucked."

He shrugs and spares me a glance and a soft smile. "Amicable, right. It did a little, but they were happier for it. Plus Mom came out, which honestly, made things easier for me."

My brows shoot high in surprise.

"I already knew I was interested in boys by then and never hid it from my parents. They were always amazing that way. Mom and Dad were best friends from school, and well, Mom sort of buried that part of herself. It made me sad as fuck when she told me."

I wince, my heart going out to Hayes and his family. "It's a story far too many people can relate to. That she reached a point where she felt able to come out, though—that's amazing." He nods as I continue, "And your dad?"

"He loved Mom, wanted her to be happy. Struggled for a while there, though."

"I can only imagine."

"Thankfully, my dad's not an asshole. He took it in his stride. It did impact their friendship, which I get. He was hurt. But they're both awesome, both remarried. I even have a kid sister who's about to turn eighteen. She'll be in college next year."

"No shit? From your mom or dad?"

"Dad." Hayes chuckles. "Dad was in his mid-forties when Hallie had Ruby."

"Oh, wow. Brave." I blink at that while also doing math to work out his dad's age. It makes me feel a hell of a lot better that he's more than a handful of years older than me.

Hayes puts the blinker on and turns left. Still not knowing the town well—even though it's my mission to study the map and learn the lay of the land for work—I recognize we're close to the sheriff's station.

"I suppose. Hallie's a few years younger than Dad. Like, ten or twelve years or something."

The information makes my heart pick up speed. I so desperately want to flick a glance at Hayes, but I'm too chickenshit. Instead, I ask, "Your mom—you said she's married?"

"Yeah. Dad moved to Denver, so not too far away. Mom's still here, in the county. Mom and Stephanie live just out of town on a large acreage. They're obsessed with rescuing strays and nursing injured animals. It's not officially a sanctuary, but they get plenty of visitors. We can head out one day, if you want? They've just taken in a gray fox. I'm planning to head out next week for a visit."

Is he asking me to meet his mom?

"Uhm… I've never seen a gray fox before," I answer a little lamely. I swear, whoever said being in your forties meant you were a grown-up didn't know what they were talking about. It's so damn easy to fall into a version of myself I haven't seen for a long time around Hayes.

I just wish it wasn't the shy, fumbling version I tended to be twenty years ago.

But shit happens, and the part of me that thinks "I don't give a fuck what people say or think" is growing a little louder every day.

When I sense movement, I glance Hayes's way. His smile is wide and warm. "In that case, let's make it a date next week. Have you got your schedule sorted for work?"

All I can do is nod. Then I realize he asked a second question, so I quickly shake my head. "Not yet. Zoey said 50 percent of my hours need to be during the usual office hours. The other 50 percent can be whenever I want." Honestly, the flexibility is amazing.

Marge did regular Monday to Friday office

hours. Not being restricted is a luxury I've never had before.

Hayes's "Well, you have access to my schedule…." is left hanging wide open.

Because, yes, I do, and I may already have considered scheduling myself around times Hayes is on duty. Obviously, not with the crazy forty-eight-hour shifts he does, but if I work the occasional weekend, that's no hardship.

"I do," I answer, our gazes connecting as he pulls up in a space in the busy parking lot.

His smile indicates he likes my answer. "You ready?" he asks, opening the door.

"I sure am." I'm genuinely excited about being here. It's young kids chasing a ball. I get that. I don't have outrageously high expectations. But it's a night out in the community. A tendril of anticipation buzzes across my skin.

It's the polar opposite of my life since leaving college, and I can't wait to start experiencing life again.

Once we're armed with hot dogs and Cokes, we settle in next to the crew. They all greet me enthusiastically and introduce me to almost everyone within hearing distance. There are a lot of names and faces, but give me a month, and I'll be hollering in the street to say hello when I spot someone I know.

Heck, on the way to our seats, we said a quick hello to Dakota, the deputy I met on scene, who's here with Tad from the bar. I may have blushed a little, wondering if Tad knew that Hayes and I left together the night we met. If Tad did, he didn't say anything. He was super friendly and simply parted ways with a smile.

The thought buoys me—the idea of settling and being part of this community— through the start of the game. Admittedly, it's slow and a little painful to watch at times, but the kids are trying, and the spectators are enthusiastic. The whole time, Hayes is at my side, a constant presence that's becoming more and more familiar.

Hayes leans in close. "You still down for drinks after this?"

It's a struggle to ignore the goose bumps from his close proximity or the warmth of his breath against my neck. "Yeah, absolutely. You're at work tomorrow, right?" I have no idea why I've asked, since I already admitted I know his schedule. It just seems like the polite thing to ask.

"Yeah, ready for the handover."

I bob my head. It means no late night for him. Or

at least that's what I assume. His early shift is also the reason I made excuses for not meeting up with him yesterday, despite him asking and me knowing he had today off. The temptation would be too much. Add in a few beers to loosen my tongue and my inhibitions, and I doubt I would have found my way home.

Not that Hayes pursuing me isn't ridiculously flattering. It is. I'm not even deliberately playing hard to get. I am legit over games. But he also knows why I'm holding back. And while he respects it, he's not deterred.

I'm happy he's not.

"Where was everyone thinking of going?" It's best I remind him—myself—we're not alone.

"Jake's." The quiet rumble of his voice sends a fresh breakout of gooseflesh to wash over my skin. Unable to resist, I pull back to look at him. Jake's is where we first met—if I ignore the vague memory I have of him as a kid. And from the heat and intensity in his gaze, he's remembering all too well exactly how that night ended.

Remy's "Whoop!" grabs our attention. Our focus snaps to the court. One of the kids from Collier's scored. We clap and cheer, and when the applause peters out, we stay looking at the court rather than each other. It gives me a moment to breathe.

To think.

To wonder why, after just one week and one earth-shattering night together, I'm easily becoming obsessed with Hayes.

Feeling my phone vibrate in my pocket, I tug it out. I open the text and smile when I see it's from Austin.

Austin: Did you survive your first week?

Me: Sure did.

Austin: Jasper wants to know how things are going with your firefighter.

A rush of warmth spreads through me, and I dart a quick glance at Hayes. Our gazes connect, his attention fully on me and what I'm doing.

"Everything okay?" His focus drifts to my phone before returning to making eye contact.

"Yeah. Just an old friend checking in and asking how I settled in at work."

Hayes smiles. "And how did your first week go?"

"Great, in all honesty. Everyone's been so welcoming," I answer while firing off a quick text to Austin that says, "All good. I'll catch up later." Putting my phone away, I turn my full attention to Hayes.

"Not sure if I'll feel quite as chilled as I have this week once Marge has left, though. She makes running everything seem so effortless."

It's been a different pace this week and a whole lot of systems for me to get my head around. A lot simpler in some ways and a lot less pressure than my old job, but what I'm doing now seems a whole lot more important.

"Marge is a powerhouse. And from what I've seen, you'll get things worked out, run them the way you want to."

Aware Zoey's sitting just a couple of seats away, I simply nod. In truth, I do have some things I'd like to tighten and a new computer program I'm interested in implementing, but I don't want to step on toes or shake things up too drastically.

At least not straightaway.

That Hayes has voiced his confidence in me is sweet. He's also pretty darn astute. Sure, he's mentioned not understanding things too well a few times, but that doesn't mean he's knowledgeable up or smarter than I think he gives himself credit for.

And that's just after a week of knowing the man.

"Thanks. I hope so. I'm determined to make it work."

He gives me a flash of a smile, and I swear happiness all but radiates off him.

Because of me. My answer.

I can't even question or doubt it when Hayes holds nothing back.

"I've got no doubt."

With that, we refocus on the game and the small humans racing around the court. There are a couple of kids who seem to have a decent skill set, which is promising. It also makes for an entertaining game when there are a couple of collisions. Though I don't think I should have snorted out a laugh at those.

Though in fairness, I'm not the only one who chuckled a time or two.

By the time the buzzer sounds and we head out, I'm keen for a softer seat and a splash of booze in a place that doesn't echo. The drive is short and barely long enough for a conversation where Hayes tells me a little about Colton, the high school teacher who's the team's coach, and a little bit more about Will, the barista from CC's.

My lips part in shock as we pull up into a parking spot, and I turn to look at Hayes. "He has a private plane?"

"Right." Hayes snorts as he shuts off the engine.

"Your expression is pretty much the same as everyone else's when we discovered that."

"Was he, like, a rock star or something?"

Hayes shakes his head. "Nah, but we do have a former Collier's resident who made it pretty big. But Will, I don't know, he was in finance or engineering or, hell"—he scratches his head and shrugs—"honestly, I have no clue. Has his own company, maybe. Whatever he used to do makes him loaded. I think he's still a partner."

"And he works in a coffee shop?"

"That's right. It's Collier's Creek, Sully. I swear this place gives folks the chance to be whoever they want to be."

It's idyllic, how he describes his town.

But I also know it's not without its problems.

I've spent some time looking over past reports of some of the incidents that the fire department has attended. Not everyone in this town is completely savory. But I suppose that makes this place more real and a little less intimidating.

"Good to know."

Hayes unclips his belt, his gaze roaming my face. The air fizzes between us—hot and electric, charged with a tension I can't quite name. The space between us is a live wire, and any movement will either close the circuit or burn us both.

He shifts slightly closer, his thigh brushing against mine. The touch is fleeting, but it sends a jolt through me like static shock. His eyes search mine, as if he's looking for something, permission, maybe, or reassurance. My breath catches in my throat, and for a beat, I think I might give in to this moment.

My thoughts whirl, a chaotic mix of desire and caution. I'm hyper-aware of every small sound—the hum of a truck's engine as it drives past us, the distant throb of music spilling from the bar, the rhythmic pounding of my own heartbeat. The air feels thick, heavy with unspoken words and possibilities.

"Do you ever miss it?" Hayes's voice is low, almost a murmur. His question catches me off guard, and I blink, trying to focus.

"Miss what?"

"Home," he says softly, his gaze steady on mine. "Where you're from."

I swallow, the intensity of his gaze making it difficult to think. "Sometimes," I admit, though the word feels inadequate. There's so much more I could say, so much more I could share, but I'm not sure I should.

His hand drifts from the steering wheel, his fingers brushing against my arm, light as a whisper. The contact is brief, almost hesitant, but it's enough to send another shiver through me. I know what this is building to, and I know how easily I could let it happen. But the thought of where that might lead makes my stomach twist. The combination of anticipation and fear is a hell of a thing.

Hayes leans in slightly, his face now inches from mine. His breath is warm against my cheek, and the smell of him—clean, with a hint of something spicy—fills my senses. The tension between us is almost unbearable, like a rubber band stretched to its limit, ready to snap.

I should say something, do something to break this moment before it spirals into something I'm not sure I'm ready for. But I'm rooted to the spot, caught between what I want and what I think is right.

He reaches up and brushes a stray lock of hair at my temple. The gesture is tender, almost intimate, and it makes my heart lurch. My resolve is slipping, my thoughts scattering like leaves in the wind. All I can think about is how close he is, how easy it would be to close the gap between us.

And then, out of nowhere, there's a sharp rap on the window. The sound is jarring, shattering the bubble we've been in. I jerk back, the spell broken, and turn to see Alice standing outside the truck, her face a mask of amusement.

Relief floods through me, mingling with a sharp stab of disappointment. I'm grateful for the interruption, but at the same time, I can't ignore the pang in my chest.

Hayes pulls back, his expression relaxed, neutral almost as he rolls down the window. "What's up, Alice?"

Alice glances between us, her gaze lingering on me for a fraction of a second longer than necessary. "Just checking in. Wanted to make sure everything's okay."

"Yeah, we're good," Hayes replies, his voice steady, though I can hear the undercurrent of something else. "Thanks."

Alice nods, but there's a flicker of curiosity in her eyes. Hell, maybe it's suspicion. It's hard to tell, and I'm too flustered to try to figure it out.

As she walks away, she yells out, "Last in gets the first round!"

I exhale slowly, trying to steady the riot of emotions churning inside me. Hayes doesn't say anything, and neither do I. The moment has passed, and I know we can't get it back.

But the weight of what almost happened lingers between us, heavy and unspoken. And I'm left knowing I need to get my shit together. I can't be *that* guy. The asshole who leads someone on. Especially when that someone is as great as Hayes.

5
PLFC

CHAPTER EIGHT

HAYES

HAVING JUST six hours of sleep means the extra-large sugar-filled coffee is justified regardless of the wide-eyed look from Cam when he made it for me. Logically, it would make more sense to head out to Mom's tomorrow, after I've had a full day's rest and a proper night's sleep. In my defense, I'm a little eager to spend time with Sully.

He worked the past couple of days, so I saw him at the firehouse. That we finally exchanged cell numbers and I spent both evenings chatting to him by text, well, that's no one's business but ours.

And today I promised him a trip to my mom's to check out the animals, and I didn't want to wait a second longer than necessary.

I pull up outside Abigail's at 2:00 p.m. on the dot.

I woke up just a half hour ago— yes, spending time with Sully is one heck of a motivator in my getting my ass moving—and I've finally stopped yawning, so it's definitely safe for me to drive. It'll mean heading home in the dark tonight, but I promised Mom and Stephanie we'd stay for dinner, so we'd be sticking around even if we'd left this morning.

My gaze immediately lands on Sully. He's outside, looking far too fucking sexy wearing my purple hat and scarf. His smile is a little crooked, showing just a hint of his teeth. It's curious how he dances between a little shy and coy to pretty damn confident.

I like that he's not predictable. It makes me feel less under the spotlight when I go off on a tangent, which I've done at least a couple of times since being around him.

He tugs open the door. "Hey."

As he settles at my side, I grin, saying, "Hey. Good day so far?" I pull away as soon as he's buckled in. He had the day off and will be back on shift in a couple of days. That his schedule aligns with mine makes me seriously happy.

"If you can call a lazy day good, then absolutely." He flashes me a smile, his gaze roaming my features. "How'd you sleep?'

"Not too bad." I bob my head as I pull off his street and head north. "I managed about six hours."

Out of the corner of my eye, I see him glance at me again. "Is that enough? That doesn't sound like a lot to me."

My lips curve high, and I risk a small glance, noticing his concerned expression. "It's plenty. We had one late-night callout, but nothing serious. I think I slept at the station for about four hours after one o'clock this morning. When you put it all together, it's a decent sleep."

He hums a little before asking, "Is that something you get used to?"

"Definitely. It's shit when you're up all night on an emergency and running on fumes, but I think every firefighter I know has learned to adapt and sleep where they're standing."

"I don't know how you do it, but it's impressive that you can. Heck, the last time I went without sleep, I was good for nothing and barely a walking, talking zombie until I got caught up."

I chuckle, imagining Sully being a little grumpy when he's tired. I bet he's adorable.

After a few beats of quiet, we're almost at the outskirts of town when he says, "So your mom's place—you said it's out of town, right?"

"Yeah, not too far. There are several small-acreage properties scattered around Collier's Creek, but the farther out you go, the larger the properties until you get a little closer to a new town."

Sully glances out the window as we reach the town line. "You know, I've never been further north than this point right here."

"No shit? Not even Canada?"

"Nope. It's on my bucket list. Have you?"

I nod. "Yeah, just once, and I definitely want to go back. I barely saw any of it."

We continue driving, the landscape opening up before us. There are a few heavyset clouds around, but the weather forecast didn't say there would be much happening today.

The farther out we go, the flat plains slowly give way to rolling hills, and in the distance, the jagged peaks of the mountain range become more pronounced against the sky. The distant mountains are draped in a fresh layer of snow that glistens under the pale sunlight filtering through the clouds. The snowcapped ridges are a deep, frosty white contrasting sharply with the dark evergreen forests clinging to their lower slopes.

"It's beautiful out here."

I glance at Sully before turning my focus ahead

and answering, "It is. It was no hardship coming home. SoCal was liberating in a way Wyoming can never truly be, but just look at this place." I love it here.

The sky above is all muted grays and soft blues, with the heavyset clouds hanging low, creating a dramatic backdrop for the rugged mountains. Honestly, as the winter sets in, it can be pretty isolating and unforgiving. This time of year, though, before winter's truly taken root, it's freakin' awe-inspiring or something.

I point into the distance about twenty-five minutes out of town where there's a collection of trees. "My mom's place is just over there."

"Are those willows?"

"Yeah. There's a large stream running west of their property. The willows love it."

"How big did you say their place was?"

"A hundred acres."

"What?" He sits up straight and looks my way. "I thought you said small."

I chuckle when I take in his wide eyes. "For around here, it is small."

"Jesus, we've got very different ideas of what constitutes small and gigantic as fuck."

My laughter bursts free, and a beautiful smile

settles on his lips when he looks my way. "Go big or go home, right?" I tease, adding in an eyebrow bounce for good measure.

"You're incorrigible."

I shrug as he continues to grin at me.

"So other than the animal shelter, what else do they do with their property?"

"They have cattle. Steph grew up out here but on a much bigger scale. Ranching is all she's ever known. I'm pretty sure she puts up with Mom's animal-rescue obsession to keep her off the tractor and away from the herd." I chuckle, thinking about Mom's good heart but what a shit farmer she makes. "Mom's a vegetarian. They have beef cattle, so she's all about balance and making their life as stress free as possible before they're sold."

"No shit? That must be interesting."

I snort. "It has been. Mom doesn't preach or any of that shit. She's more focused on her health and animal welfare. But she's been known to drive Steph to distraction a time or twenty."

I turn off onto a smaller road leading to several properties stacked against one another. Mom and Stephanie's ranch is the sixth along, so we're not too far away. It's just enough time to tell Sully about the infamous "Winter Cow Roundup" a few years back.

"So, Mom's a bit of a character."

We make eye contact, and I swear his gaze softens. "She already sounds awesome, and having a personality is what it's all about, right?"

"Oh, you have no idea," I say, chuckling. "Okay, so it's a freezing February morning—snow on the ground, wind screaming like it's trying to rip the barn doors off. Mom decides she *needs* to check on the cattle, make sure they're doing okay in the cold."

"Doesn't sound so bad." Sully shrugs.

"Except, like I told you, Mom's a vegetarian and barely tolerates the idea of raising cattle for beef. Her heart's in the right place, but… well, she's not exactly a rancher. That's Steph's territory. Anyway, Steph told her the cows were fine, but you know how people get these ideas in their heads?"

He nods, amusement crossing his features as he looks at me.

I turn back to the road, seeing their property up ahead. "Mom was convinced they were freezing or starving or something."

"So what happened?"

"Well, I'm inside, enjoying my coffee. I can't remember why I was there. Maybe for Mom's birthday. Or it could have been something else." I pause, trying to think of why I was there that morning. Maybe I'd stayed overnight for some—

Sully's gentle "So I'm assuming they weren't freezing or starving" reminds me to get back on track.

"Right, so I see Mom out there, bundled up like a marshmallow, scarf practically swallowing her face, and she's heading into the pasture with a bag of feed —like she's about to save the day."

Sully raises an eyebrow. I quickly glance away. He's so easy to look at and has the best facial expressions.

"I'm watching from the window, and Steph's out there, too, waving her arms, trying to get Mom to stop. But Mom, she's on a mission. Doesn't listen. Next thing you know, she's right in the middle of the herd. Now, Mom might know how to handle stray cats and dogs and even the occasional fox or moose—well, sort of. I'll tell you about Fred the moose sometime—but forty head of cattle? Not so much."

Sully laughs. "Oh shit. So, it didn't go as planned?"

"Not even close," I say, grinning. "The cows all come toward her like she's some kind of feed goddess. And Mom, in her finite wisdom—I think that's what Steph called it—decides to dump the entire bag on the ground in one big heap."

Sully is cracking up now. "You're kidding? That sounds kind of dangerous."

"I wish I was, and it definitely is dangerous. Even I know that. Seriously, there's a reason why my favorite cow is a big-ass medium-rare fillet. Anyhow, feed went *everywhere*. The cows, all forty of them, start charging for the food. Mom's right in the middle, dodging hooves, dancing around so she doesn't get trampled. Meanwhile, Steph's standing there, ready to lose it, yelling for Mom to get out of there."

"What did your mom do?" Sully asks, barely containing his laughter.

"She starts *laughing*—like, this pure, fucking epic laugh—as the cows are circling her like she's some kind of snow queen with a magical bag of feed. Steph had to wade through the snow to pull Mom out of the mess, and by the end of it, Mom's still giggling, convinced she made a 'special connection' with the cows."

Sully's laughter is deep and loud. "Sounds like your mom's a handful."

I smile, warmth flooding my belly. "She is, but you'll love her. She's got a big heart. And now you'll see why Steph keeps her as far away from the cattle as possible."

At that, we reach the gate to their property.

"Is this it?"

"Sure is," I answer. I love this place. Not that I'd want to live this far out of town or spend time ranching, but I can appreciate how beautiful it is.

The cattle grid rumbles under my tires as we cross it. I follow the gravel driveway up to their small ranch. It's a cute thing, not too big. It's not a sprawling ranch or anything. They do have a small cabin that I tend to stay in on the odd occasion I sleep over. It's set up for the times they get a worker in for a few weeks, usually when calving or they've got a big fencing job or something.

My grin is instant when my gaze falls on Mom. "There she is." She's practically buried in an oversized coat, but it's the bright yellow woolly hat that makes me snicker. It was the first thing I knitted, and it didn't go exactly as planned. Mom insisted on keeping it and loves it still.

A few years in, the thing hasn't unraveled, so I can't have done too bad of a job, despite its flaws.

I push open the truck door, but before I barrel out, I stop in my tracks, remembering this is one of the times I need to step up and not get distracted. Immediately, I check on Sully.

The smile he's aimed at me is reassuring.

"You okay?" I need to be certain. My mind-reading skills are for shit.

"Yeah." He flicks a glance at Mom, a thick swallow following. As he does so, my eyes widen as awareness slams into me.

Sully is meeting my mom and stepmom.

That's some next-level serious shit right here. That I didn't even realize the significance before doesn't even surprise me.

Before I can part my lips to reassure Sully that there's no pressure and we really are here to see the cute fox, a double "oh shit" whammy smacks me right between the eyes.

Here's the thing.... I'm close with my folks—my mom especially. Over the years she's helped me through practically every crisis I've had. We're also a family of oversharers.

"So I might have told my mom that we hooked up and who you are and that we're working togeth-er." The words spill out of me at warp speed. I've never been good at holding myself back or hiding what's on my mind.

That's a good thing. Or I thought it was until Sully chokes on nothing—air, I suspect, going down the wrong tube—and splutters, his face turning the same shade as the jersey my favorite football team wears.

"Uhm… shit." I lift my arm, about to pat his back, but Sully waves me off. "Okay, as long as you're not going to die on me."

He drags in a lungful of air, finally getting his breathing under control. Watery eyes peer over at me as he says, "I'm fine. Honest, I'm fine." The wheezing makes me suspect he's exaggerating, but he's speaking, so I'm not *as* worried.

"You sure?"

"Uh-huh." A shuddery exhale follows, and Sully's gaze is back on me. "Just warn a guy next time. Abigail's always going on about the likelihood of me having a heart attack."

I blanch. "You're high-risk for a heart attack?" Shit, does he take pills or something? That's a detail I should know, right? Or maybe not. Fuck, I don't know.

"No, Hayes. Shit, no. I'm not high-risk or anything." He gives a reassuring squeeze of my forearm, and I relax into his touch. "The only thing I'm at risk of is having a big sister who nags and reminds me how important it is to exercise. And maybe choking on nothing is a risk factor." Another squeeze of my arm and he smiles.

The panic on his face has completely cleared, and my pulse is calming, thank fuck.

"Okay." I nod, easing out a breath while shifting my arm so I'm holding his hand instead. Sully's eyes widen a fraction, but he doesn't let go.

"So you told your folks about me?" He angles his head and flicks his gaze out of the window before looking back at me.

Right—Mom.

She's used to having to wait for me to get myself together. She'll be fine for a couple more minutes. She won't even think this is strange, me sitting here talking to Sully despite having spent the car ride together.

I bob my head. "I did."

His brows lift, and he stares at me silently. After a beat, I figure he's expecting more.

"Right, so, yeah. I told Mom about you. She's looking forward to meeting you." I hesitate, but fuck it. I really like Sully, seriously *like him* like him.

After witnessing my parents' divorce and the secret Mom held back, I decided a long time ago that if I met someone, I'd be honest to a fault. I have no idea what "to a fault" actually means, but I've heard it said a few times about me, and only a handful of those were with a wince. I figure it can't be a completely bad thing.

"The fox is super cute, and I thought you might like to cuddle it," I start, thinking about the photos Mom has texted me. "But you meeting Mom and Steph is great too. I like us spending time together. I like it just as much as us hooking up, and I'm definitely open to more of that."

His eyes widen, but he still doesn't pull away.

"Often. Regularly," I clarify. *Double fuck it.* "Exclusively." I lift my right shoulder, trying to fend off the bubble of embarrassment starting to grow in my gut.

If Sully only wants to be friends—work colleagues won't cut it—I'll find a way to make peace with that. But after two weeks of spending time with him, getting to know him, I'm already thinking about the what-ifs and sunshine and rainbows and possibilities of us together. Plus, our one hot night together is wedged in my mind, refusing to fade away.

Everyone knows my addiction is sugar. Sully, though? Man, he tastes like sugar. No. Better than sugar. Who the fuck would have thought that was possible?

Sully shifts his gaze away from me and to the

front window. My gut clenches. Is that his answer? His response? Is he simply dismissing—

"It's snowing."

"What?" I shake my head and follow his gaze, my eyes widening in surprise. "No shit. It is snowing." That wasn't in the forecast. I jerk my head around, remembering Mom is still outside. "Shit, we better go in before Mom turns into a snowwoman."

With a nod of agreement, Sully releases my hand. I don't like it, but it is what it is. What I like even less is that he never said anything after I spilled what's in my heart. Not that he really had much of a chance.

But why didn't he say anything? I can't shake the doubt creeping in. I know he's not the type to shy away from a conversation. Maybe he's just as surprised by what I said as I am. Or maybe he's still processing what Hayes told him. I can't help but wonder if he's thinking about that conversation and if it's lingering in his mind, the same way it is in mine.

Plus, I think as I jump out of the truck, grabbing my coat as I do, it's likely I blindsided him. Which I'm pretty sure is a football term. It came from that movie with Quinton Aaron and Sandra Bullock.

Maybe. Who knows?

But yeah, I think I surprised him.

I check on Sully before darting to greet Mom. He closes the truck door, tugs on his coat, still wearing the hat and scarf I gifted him, and makes his way around the hood to me.

"Hurry your asses up. It's colder than a witch's tit out here!" Mom hollers.

I snicker, my chest warming when Sully huffs out a laugh beside me.

We pick up the pace and reach Mom, who wraps me in a hug. Her embrace is firm and familiar, but I pull away quicker than normal, not wanting Sully to be out in the snow that's already covering his shoulders.

"Let's get inside so you can meet Sully properly," I say.

Mom's eyes widen a little, and I roll mine. What, I can't be thoughtful?

"Come on in. The fire's going and the coffee's hot," Steph says from the open doorway. Her grin is wide.

I smile back before reaching out to Sully, putting my palm on the small of his back as we head up the few steps onto the porch. Once under the porch roof, I untie my boots, and Sully does the same.

"Where should I put these?" he asks, indicating his boots.

"Let me." I take them off him and store them away in the shoe cabinet Mom and Steph keep out here.

"Thanks."

"Coffee, then fox cuddles?" I ask with a smile. Mom's already inside with Steph, leaving the two of us alone.

He smiles back, eagerness in his expression. It's good to see the uncertainty gone. "Definitely."

I hesitate, wanting desperately to take his hand. Being a bit much, a little full-on is kind of my thing. Or so I've been told. That awareness makes me keep my hands to myself. My fingers twitch, but I double on down with my self-control.

With a nod, I indicate for Sully to get out of the cold. He does so, and I close the door behind us. Heat immediately envelops us, so I make quick work of stowing away our coats, hats, and scarves before leading him into the kitchen, following the scent of coffee.

CHAPTER NINE

SULLY

My ass is killing me sitting on the wooden floorboards, but I don't have it in me to drag myself away. It's not even to do with my potential mortification of creaky bones and achy moans when I get up in front of Hayes.

No. It has everything to do with the adorable gray fox who's so affectionate, I'm seriously considering ways to smuggle him away.

Jayne, Hayes's mom, told me the baby fox is just five weeks old. The poor thing was found about a week back by a local. Its mom was lame, so the kindest thing to do was put it down, which left two babies. One had been too malnourished to save, so that left this little guy.

I stroke the fox's soft fur and glance up to find

Hayes leaning against the kitchen counter. He's watching me, a lazy grin on his face, arms folded across his chest. I catch his eyes flicking to where my legs are awkwardly folded beneath me, like he's waiting for me to give up and ask for help getting off the floor.

"I'm going to need a forklift to get me up," I mutter, half to myself, half to the fox. The little guy nuzzles into my hand, clearly uninterested in my plight.

"You know," Hayes says, pushing off the counter and strolling toward me, "I think you've got a future as a fox whisperer. My mom's gonna be jealous."

I roll my eyes, but I'm smiling despite myself. "Please, your mom's the one who has a way with animals. I just happen to be the closest warm body."

Hayes crouches down beside me, close enough that his knee brushes against my thigh. It's a small touch, but my skin warms from the contact. His hand moves to join mine in lightly stroking the fox's back. "I dunno. He seems pretty attached to you. Maybe he's trying to tell you something."

I raise an eyebrow, keeping my voice light. "Like what? 'Take me home with you'?"

"Could be," Hayes says, his voice lower now. "Or

maybe he's saying you belong out here, in Collier's. With him. With… us."

There's a beat of silence, and I pretend to focus on the fox. The weight of Hayes's words hangs between us. I've been trying to convince myself that starting something with him would be a bad idea. But every time he looks at me like this, every time he touches me, it gets harder to hold on to that belief.

I clear my throat, willing my voice to stay steady. "You're gonna make me sound like I'm collecting strays. First, a fox. Next, a puppy."

Hayes grins, his gaze sliding to meet mine. "Maybe that's not a bad idea. You've got space now that you live out of the city, right? So what's stopping you?"

"I don't know," I say honestly, though obviously I need my own home first. "I've never really had pets. I've always been too busy or lived in places where it didn't make sense. But…." I trail off, thinking about my new life here, the quiet that's both comforting and a little overwhelming. "It might be nice."

Hayes shifts closer, his arm grazing mine as he reaches over to scratch the fox behind its ears. "I had a dog, growing up," he says, his tone softening. "Old golden retriever named Buddy. He was the best.

Always followed me around, slept on the foot of my bed…. God, I loved that dog."

His voice is warm, nostalgic, and I relax even further, drawn in by the glimpse of his childhood. "Sounds like a good companion."

"Yeah," Hayes says, his eyes lingering on me. "He was. You know, pets make a place feel like home. Not that I'm trying to sell you on the idea, but… I don't think it'd be a bad thing for you. To have something waiting for you at home."

There's a quiet sincerity in his words, and for a moment, I let myself imagine it. Coming home from work to a dog. A routine that's not about rushing to meet some deadline but enjoying the slower pace of life here. It's… tempting.

"What about you?" I ask, turning the question back on him. "You ever think about getting another dog?"

Hayes shrugs, but there's a gleam in his eye. "Maybe one day. But I'd have to find someone willing to help out with it. Dogs need attention, you know."

I bite back a laugh, shaking my head at his not-so-subtle flirtation. "So, this is your plan? Convince me to get a dog so you can hang around more?"

He flashes me the crooked grin that always seems

to disarm me. "Well, I wasn't gonna say it outright, but… if the shoe fits."

I shake my head, unable to stop the smile tugging at my lips. "You're impossible."

"Impossible or charming?" he asks, leaning in just enough that I feel the warmth of his breath on my cheek.

My heart skips a beat, and for a second, I can't think of a clever reply. I glance toward the kitchen, where Jayne and her wife are busying themselves with dinner, chatting away but very much within earshot. This whole thing—being here with Hayes, his mom knowing about us, the way he's so openly flirting—it's starting to feel super real.

"I don't know," I murmur, turning back to the fox in my lap. "You tell me."

Hayes's hand brushes mine again, lingering just long enough to make it clear that he's not backing off anytime soon. "I think you're figuring it out."

The tension between us crackles, but it's the kind of tension that feels more like anticipation than anything else. I know I should probably say something to deflect, to remind him—or myself—of why this is a bad idea. But sitting here with this fox, Hayes so close, his playful smile softening into something more sincere… it doesn't feel like a bad idea at all.

And that's what scares me the most. Though, to be fair, my fear is starting to feel a little more like nervous excitement. Like possibility.

"Michael, honey."

Hayes whips his head up and peers over at his mom. "Yeah, Mom?"

Knowing just how this looks, a blush hits my cheeks.

"You need to think about staying the night. The snow's coming down fast and heavy."

I peer out the window as Steph adds, "I'm not sure how much we can trust the forecast, since they got this snow dump wrong, but it looks like it's not likely to die off until early in the morning. It won't be fun driving in it, that's for sure."

Visibility is pretty bad. I can't even see Hayes's truck.

But staying here…? Not going to lie, it feels awkward. But better awkward than being out in this weather, right?

Still beside me on the hard floor—I really do need to get up soon, as my ass is numb—Hayes makes eye contact as he asks, "What do you think?"

"I trust you to make the right call," I say with a

shrug. "This whole whiteout thing is new to me. If I were by myself, not a chance I'd attempt to drive in it. Hell, I'm dreading driving in the snow to get to work from my sister's."

"You haven't driven in the snow before?"

I shake my head.

"I'll give you a few lessons." He nods as though he's settling on a plan.

"You will, huh?" Amusement trickles into my tone. I swear, it's easy to forget he's so many years younger than I am. To be fair, that only happens sometimes. Though, in truth, when he gets distracted and goes off on tangents, I suspect that's a Hayes thing and has nothing to do with his age.

Hell, the man's in his thirties. He's not a child.

Plus there's the whole firefighter hero thing he has going for him.

A sheepish expression appears along with a shy smile. "Uhm, would you like for me to give you a few lessons sometime?"

He's sweet as hell. "Yeah. That'd be great."

His smile expands, so bright and genuine that I melt a little more. Hayes is impossible not to fall for.

"Okay, great. Perhaps next week, we can—"

Steph clearing her throat pulls him up short.

"Right, so yeah, are you okay to stay the night?" he asks me. "It might be best. It's already going dark."

I nod, more than okay with that despite the flutter of nerves coming to life in my gut.

"Perfect." Steph claps her hands, drawing our attention to her. She's smiling at her stepson with complete affection. "You'll both be in the cabin."

Hayes shifts uncomfortably at my side. He parts his lips as though to speak.

"The spare bedroom in the house is a disaster." His mom sounds positively gleeful. "It's become little more than a dumping ground—"

"Animal sanctuary is probably more appropriate," Steph tags on.

"I'll just be grateful to have somewhere warm and a bed to sleep in, thank you." I saw the cabin earlier. It's cozy but has a chimney, so I'm assuming it'll be warm.

"Great. Now that's settled, how about we get ready to eat? Sully, we've made sure every single tree nut is out of sight."

My eyes widen at that. Though, I don't know why. Time and time again, Hayes has proven to be incredibly thoughtful. "Thank you. I appreciate it."

She smiles before turning to her son. "Michael,

you want to show Sully where the bathroom is to wash up?"

"Sure thing, Mom." He jumps up, ridiculously agile. He takes the cute fox from me and places him in the small crate near the fire. Meanwhile, I'm mentally preparing myself to move and willing my limbs to behave.

I've got this. Clumsily and with no grace, most likely, but I've definitely—

"Here." Hayes's palm appears before me, urging me to grasp and hold on.

Like fuck am I letting him lift me up. Sure, he may have seen me naked, but pulling my ass up off the floor means he'll figure out just how many extra pounds I'm carrying, or worse, how I grunt and groan when gravity decides to be particularly cruel. I hesitate, looking at his hand like it's a challenge I'm not quite ready to take on.

"I'm fine," I say, though even I can hear the reluctance in my voice. I brace my palms against the floor, trying to push myself up, but I can already tell this is going to end badly.

Hayes doesn't say a word. He just tilts his head, one eyebrow raised like he's not buying a second of my resistance. Before I can protest again, his hand grips mine firmly, and in one smooth, effortless motion, he pulls me up.

It's… easy. Too easy. The kind of easy that makes my brain go quiet because I've been so focused on dreading the humiliation that I'm not prepared for how quickly I'm back on my feet, face-to-face with him. Barely an inch between us.

I don't have time to feel embarrassed. Not when I'm close enough to smell his scent—something fresh and woodsy, like soap and a hint of smoke from the fire. It's intoxicating.

My hand is still in his.

I should let go, take a step back, make some space between us, but I don't. Neither of us moves. Hayes is looking at me, that playful grin from earlier replaced by something quieter, more intent. I can feel the heat of his body, his steady presence filling the space around us.

"You good?" he asks, his voice low, soft, like he, too, is suddenly aware of how close we are.

I nod, but I don't entirely trust myself to speak just yet. I'm too aware of him—of the warmth of his hand in mine, of the way his eyes seem to flicker between mine, searching for… something.

"You sure?" he teases, though there's something

behind his words that lingers, like he's asking about more than just whether I'm steady on my feet.

"Yeah," I manage, finally releasing his hand, but the sensation of it stays with me longer than I want to admit. "I'm good."

"Good." Hayes's smile softens, and he steps back, giving me space to breathe, though I already miss the closeness.

I clear my throat, trying to shake off the remaining tension. "Lead the way, then."

He shoots me one last look—something knowing, like he's fully mindful of the effect he has on me —before turning toward the hallway. I follow, trying to focus on anything other than the fact that being close to him is becoming harder and harder to resist.

And that's something I can't afford to dwell on right now.

Not when my gaze keeps drifting to his ass and how fine he looks in his Wranglers. Jesus, jeans like that should be illegal. They cup his ass, making me envious of the fabric. I'm lucky enough to know what his butt looks like in the flesh, what it feels like in my palms.

My dick stirs, and I snap my attention away immediately, only to make eye contact with Steph.

Her lips are clamped between her teeth, and amusement is alight in her gaze.

I'm busted. Completely, humiliatingly busted.

But hell, Hayes's ass is delectable.

Ignoring the heat creeping up my neck, I simply shrug, feigning just how carefree I feel when I really want the floor to open up and swallow me whole.

When she snorts and shakes her head, her amusement obvious, I figure I'm in the clear. I pick up my pace and join Hayes to wash up for dinner.

"Fuck, it's freezing."

Another "no shit, Sherlock" moment, I suspect, but it's impossible to ignore just how cold it is. The small cabin is probably a hundred yards from the main house, but it feels like I've got shards of ice slicing into me with every yard.

The snow hasn't let up, but it has changed. It's no longer pretty and fluffy. With the increased wind, it's like tiny daggers of freezing glass being propelled our way. Only a slight exaggeration, but if we don't get inside soon, either my nose or my dick is going to drop off.

Heck, maybe both.

Hayes chuckles at my side, not seeming the least bit perturbed by the Titanic-iceberg level of cold it is. "It's barely November."

"Meaning?" I ask as our feet finally hit the small wooden porch of the cabin.

"Meaning, Sully, if you think this is cold, we're going to have to get you one of those sleeping-bag coats to survive when the winter really hits."

I glance at his expression as he pushes open the door. Shit, he's not joking. He's amused for sure, but he's telling the truth. As the warmth of the house wraps around me—Hayes lit the fire about an hour ago—I don't have it in me to care right now.

All I want is to heat up in front of the incredible fire blazing in the cute hearth in the corner of the small, open-plan room.

I tug off my coat, taking it all in.

It's rustic but clearly well cared for. The furniture is well-worn and looks super comfortable. There's a flat-screen TV on the wall, so while there's an old charm to the place, it's fitted with all the modern conveniences both in the sitting area and the kitchen.

"The bathroom's through there." Hayes points

toward a closed door. "The water pressure is great. Steph fitted a new pump last year. The hot-water system is awesome too."

"A hot shower is tempting."

Hayes swipes his tongue over his bottom lip—just the tip and just enough to make it crystal clear he's thinking of me naked in the shower. I might feel like I'm in a little over my head with Hayes due to the whole drop-dead-gorgeous factor and the my-nephew's-best-friend reality, which still makes me wince, but I've been around the block a few times, and I know what chemistry looks and feels like.

The thing with Hayes, though, is that I'm not sure I've felt it quite so strongly before.

That doesn't hold me back from asking, "The bedroom?"

He rubs his palm over the back of his neck, a hint of unease in his posture. I raise my brows in surprise at his reaction. Hayes is the epitome of confidence. Cocky, almost.

"Well, one of the couches turns into a bed." He gives a one-shoulder shrug.

I press my lips together, understanding immediately what he's avoided saying until now. "And the bedroom?"

He searches my expression. Whatever he sees has his shoulders relaxing a fraction and a dangerously sexy smirk forming. "One extra-comfortable bed that's big enough for two."

I huff out a laugh, relishing the lightness of how easy it is to tease and flirt with Hayes.

"How about you find me that change of clothes you promised me, let me shower, and we'll figure it out?" I'm bullshitting the both of us. Of course I'm going to share a bed with him. What's more is, I have no plans to keep my hands to myself either.

Hayes is completely responsible for my actions and lack of control.

From the moment he collected me early this afternoon, he's showed me the kind of attention that's kept my heart beating fast while somehow simultaneously making me feel at ease and comfortable. And don't even get me started on how he's taken every opportunity to touch me, care for me, and get to know me better.

I've lapped up his attention like a starving man, and I can't kid myself that he's just on a mission to get me riding his cock. He absolutely doesn't *just* want that. The last time was explosive, and I hope to find out very soon how much better the second time will be.

But back to his thoughtfulness, his kindness… that's all him, Hayes, the man who's as gorgeous inside as he is in his uniform and naked. Meeting his mom simply confirmed that.

"Okay." His tone is gruff, a level deeper than it was a moment ago. "Do you want dessert when you get out?"

My smile is wide. My laugh is loud.

A frown appears when he takes in my reaction, confusion dancing in his expression, but it's only there for a few seconds before, once again, a sweet pink touches his cheeks. Yeah, I have little doubt he remembers where his last offer of dessert got us.

"So, is that a yes?"

Gravel. Sinful, delectable gravel. Goose bumps appear on my arms, and I swallow hard, the gulp audible despite the crackling fire.

Bolstered by the heat in his gaze and the zap of combustible awareness between us, I step into his space.

Nothing this good can be wrong. I know it deep in my gut.

It's tempting to lean in and capture his mouth, but if I do, we won't stop. I'll be flat on my back or on my knees. Either way sounds phenomenal, but first, I really want to shower. If I prep, too, well, the quicker we can blow each other's minds.

"That's a 'dust off whatever bottle of lube you have squirreled away here, and I'll be back in ten minutes.'" With a racing pulse and a shaky breath, I step back.

Before I escape into the bathroom, Hayes calls my name. I glance over my shoulder at him, drinking the man in. Fuck, he's beautiful. "Yeah?"

"Let's not bother with the change of clothes." With that, he unbuckles his belt and undoes the button on his jeans.

Fuck.

It takes every ounce of my willpower to get myself in the bathroom, but I do so, knowing it'll be worth it. Hayes makes me feel sexy and wanted, and *I* want to be able to relax into each touch tonight.

Now that I've made up my mind that I don't want to keep pretending, I want it all.

I make fast work of cleaning myself up. By the time I'm done, my skin is pink, my face is flushed, and my hard cock is jutting out, ready for attention.

I take a quick look in the mirror and a shaky breath. My eyes are bright, a little wild, and fuck if that doesn't give me the boost I need to push away any insecurities I have about my soft stomach.

A few steps later, I find Hayes in the bedroom. On top of the sheets, legs slightly parted and completely naked, he really does look like my wet dream come to life. He's cupping his balls, playing gently, and doesn't stop when his gaze lands on me.

"Remind me to ask to see those calendars." I quirk my brow. Sure, I'm teasing, but I definitely want to get my hands on every single charity calendar he's featured in. I wonder if I can get back copies.

He chuckles, his heated gaze unwavering. "Even when you're the only one to get the real thing?"

A Big-Dipper-sized drop happens in my gut.

The only one.

His words are heady. They're also all I need to get my ass moving and on the bed.

I don't overthink. I focus on how he makes me feel and what I want to do to this man.

The teasing between us is easy, familiar, charged with the kind of playfulness that only comes from knowing each other intimately. Hayes's grin widens as I crawl up the bed toward him, grazing my fingers along the edge of the sheet before dipping them lower to trail against the inside of his thigh. His skin is warm, goose bumps following in the wake of my touch.

He shifts, still cupping himself lazily but allowing me access, like he's offering up his body as a gift. "Do you always like to take your time?" he murmurs, voice low, laced with amusement. "You going to make me beg?"

"Wouldn't dream of it." My smirk doesn't hide the heat rising inside me. I slide my hand higher, brushing his cock with just enough pressure to tease. He lets out a soft, content sigh, the sound like music to my ears.

"Good," he groans, arching a little as I stroke him with more intent. His hand falls away, giving me full rein over him. "I don't think I could handle the waiting. Two weeks is already more than I can bear."

There's a familiar thrill in hearing his need, in knowing exactly what to do to drive him wild. Leaning over, I drag my tongue up his chest, tasting the salt of his skin before capturing his lips in a deep, slow kiss. His fingers tangle in my hair, pulling me closer as his hips rise instinctively, desperate for more contact.

"Impatient?" I murmur against his mouth, still playing with him, tracing the length of his shaft, knowing just when to tighten my grip to elicit that sweet gasp I love.

"You're cruel," he pants, though there's no real

bite to his words. His body betrays him, pushing into my touch, seeking more. "But damn, you're worth it."

I chuckle, feeling his chest rise and fall under mine as I kiss a path down his body, nipping at the sensitive spots I plan to memorize. His muscles tense under my lips, a quiet whimper escaping as I take him fully in hand. I love how responsive he is, how he gives himself over without hesitation. My control over him, the way he trusts me, makes the heat between us almost unbearable.

The sound of the lube cap clicking open is met with a low, drawn-out moan from Hayes. His head falls back against the pillow, eyes half lidded as he watches me slick my hand. "Fuck, you look good like that," he breathes. His voice is rough, almost reverent.

"Like what?"

"Like you know exactly what you're doing. Like you're in control, and I'm just along for the ride."

The corner of my mouth quirks up at his words. "Maybe you are."

I don't give him time to respond before I take him into my mouth, his length sliding between my lips as I work his base with my hand. His whole body tenses, fingers tightening in my hair as he lets out a strangled groan. His taste, his scent, the way his muscles flex and shudder—it's all intoxicating, and I know he's on the edge.

Hayes shifts beneath me, a tremor running through his frame as I hollow my cheeks, increasing the pressure. His breathing is ragged, the slick sounds of my mouth on him mingling with his soft curses. The way he's trying so hard to hold on only drives me to push him further, slipping my fingers lower, tracing the sensitive area behind his balls before pressing them inside him.

"Shit—" His breath hitches as I work him, finding the rhythm that I hope will make him fall apart. "I can't—"

"You can," I whisper, pulling back just enough to meet his eyes. The desperation there, the need, sends a rush of heat straight to my core. "I've got you."

And then, with an agonizing slowness, I start to move. Each thrust of my fingers, each glide of my mouth, is deliberate, calculated. He bucks against me, lost in the pleasure, and I can feel him getting closer, his entire body strung tight like a bow.

Just as he's about to tip over the edge, I stop, pulling away with a smirk that earns me a frustrated growl. "Fuck," he gasps, half laughing, half begging.

"I love watching you come undone," I answer, my voice rough with my own need. I kiss him again, slow and deep, and his lips move against mine with a hunger that mirrors my own.

He flips me onto my back with a growl, and before I can catch my breath, he's over me, his cock brushing against my entrance along with lubed fingers I didn't even realize he'd slicked.

"You prepped." Awe colors his words and sends a fresh bolt of need to my cock. His gaze locks with mine, intense and dark, and I nod, giving him the permission he doesn't need but asks for anyway.

With one slow thrust, he's inside me, and I gasp, gripping his shoulders as he fills me completely. There's no hesitation now, no teasing—just the raw, unrelenting need between us. Hayes moves with a rhythm that's wild, his breath hot against my neck as he murmurs praises and curses into my ear.

I'm lost in him, in the way he feels, in the way his body fits perfectly with mine. Each thrust sends waves of pleasure coursing through me, and I can barely hold on, the pressure building, coiling tighter and tighter until I'm right on the brink.

"Come for me," he whispers, his lips brushing my ear. His voice is low, commanding, and it's all I need. I let go, my release crashing over me as his follows, our bodies moving together in perfect harmony.

We collapse in a tangle of limbs, breathless and

spent, the room filled with the sounds of our ragged breathing. He presses a soft kiss to my forehead, his hand still resting possessively on my hip.

"I think I might keep you," he murmurs, and I can't help the smile that spreads across my face.

"Okay," I reply, knowing there's nowhere else I'd rather be than right here with him.

5
F LPC

CHAPTER TEN

HAYES

ONCE A MONTH we run a training session, bringing together our two full-time units and the volunteers. It's often a fun night. We spend a couple of hours refreshing our skills, which is followed by a catch-up and usually ends with us tossing back a few beers— except for the four on-duty firefighters and the four volunteers on call.

I'm off duty, and tonight's shaping up the same way as usual. The only difference is, Sully's here, and I'm struggling to keep my attention off him, let alone my hands off him.

We're on the last refresher task—a hose drill, of all things. It's fairly simple, something everyone with the slightest bit of training can do, even the volunteers who don't get as much practice. I glance at

Sully, who's fidgeting slightly next to the rig. He's in his element as the firehouse office manager, but this… this is way out of his comfort zone—even though he insisted on joining in, thinking it was a good idea to get to know the team.

Dean Hobart, the major's brother, was chatting with him earlier. After a ball of jealousy tried to take hold, I'd quickly gotten over myself—probably because of the crooked smile Sully gave me as I walked by. It's great that the team is getting to know him, and Dean's a good guy.

But I swear, every time I'm close to Sully, I feel that familiar flutter in my chest.

"All right, Sully, let's see you handle the hose," I tease lightly, making sure my tone stays encouraging.

His eyes widen, and he looks at the coiled hose like it's a rattlesnake. "I've got it," he says, though he looks unsure, a little stiff in his movements. He steps forward, clearly trying his best. I'm proud of him. He's really putting himself out there.

But before Sully can even start, Dave—a volunteer with a history of overconfidence and a smug grin that's way too familiar—speaks up. "Careful, Sully," he says, loud enough for everyone to hear.

"Don't pull a muscle. We're not doing paperwork here, buddy."

Laughter ripples through the group, but my eyes narrow. Dave's always had this cocky attitude. We hooked up once, when I was fresh out of high school, but that was a mistake I regretted almost immediately. He's been flirting on and off ever since I returned to Collier's, never quite catching on—or maybe just refusing to acknowledge—that I'm not interested.

Tonight, it's different. Dave isn't just being his usual annoying self. He's testing me, picking up on something. My interest in Sully maybe. It's like he can sense it. That or I really am doing a crappy job of hiding how Sully lights up my world.

"Cut it out, Dave." I keep my voice sharp but steady. The laughter dies down. "We're here to train and support one another."

Dave gives me a look, one eyebrow raised like he's surprised by the bite in my tone. I'm sure he's not the only one—I'm a little surprised myself.

"Relax, it's just a joke," he says, his grin faltering for a second.

"Uh-huh," I reply coolly, my eyes locking with his. He might not realize it yet, but the days of him getting away with this are over. Sully doesn't need shit.

There's a brief pause, tension settling into the air. Sully stands there, frozen, and I can feel his surprise. For a second, I worry that I've embarrassed him. But when he glances at me, there's a small, grateful nod before he smiles.

Sully's eyes flicker between Dave and the hose, and then he takes a deep breath. With a quick smile, he looks at the hose like it's some wild creature, raising his hands in mock surrender. "I think I'll survive this round without a workers' comp claim," he says, his voice light but just loud enough for the group to catch. His eyes widen comically as he adds, "But hey, if I do pull a muscle, I'll make sure to fill out the paperwork in triplicate—just to be thorough."

A ripple of laughter spreads, even from Dave, who snorts despite himself. The tension breaks, the chuckles bouncing around the group, and even I feel the knot in my stomach ease a little.

Sully grins and takes a confident step forward, the stiffness gone as he begins to handle the hose with a steady hand. He shoots me a quick, playful glance, like he's saying, "I've got this."

A still-smirking Dave seems to deflate slightly,

the sharpness in his attitude dulled. "Fair enough," he mutters, but there's a hint of respect in his voice now. He does keep his distance for the rest of the session, though. I catch him eyeing me a few times, and it's clear what he's thinking. He knows something's up between Sully and me. But that's my business, not his.

As the session wraps up and we start putting away gear, Sully drifts over to me, his face a mix of exhaustion and relief. "Thanks for letting me join in," he says quietly, his eyes meeting mine with that soft, endearing look that's been pulling me in since day one.

"Always," I reply, giving him a gentle nudge. I want to reach out and touch him—just a quick brush of my hand on his arm—but I hold back. We're still keeping this under wraps, and with Dave lurking nearby, I'm not about to give him more fuel for his teasing.

Sully lingers for a second longer, his gaze flicking toward the others before returning to me. "Watching you play the hero is kinda hot," he adds, his voice low, a playful smile tugging at his lips.

"Watching you not take shit is even hotter," I say, trying to keep my tone casual, but my mind's already racing ahead to when we'll finally be alone again.

We break apart as the guys start heading toward the communal area, ready for that end-of-session catch-up. I follow along, but my mind is still half with Sully, wondering where we stand. Is he my boyfriend? Or are we just… something undefined?

I don't have an answer yet, but I know one thing for sure: I'm not letting Dave—or anyone else—ruin what's happening between us.

I grab myself a beer, noting Sully already has one. With my bottle in hand, I sit next to him. I figure it's better this way, less obvious than me mooning over him from afar. There are already a few conversations going on; one is about the tree-lighting ceremony taking place in town in a couple of weeks.

"Are you going to be selling your calendars?" Dean asks me, earning a chuckle from the group as well as groans and eye rolls.

"Don't get him started," Alice says, holding her beer up in cheers before taking a sip.

I flip her off. "Don't worry, Alice. I've got your ten set aside. Nothing to be embarrassed about that you want so many."

She snorts. "I'll get my darts ready, and the modesty stickers. Last thing I want is to be looking at your hairy nips."

A loud laugh huffs out of me. "From the hundred

back copies you own of the previous *three* calendars I've been featured in—"

That gets me a heap of balled-up papers—and a few potato chips too—thrown in my direction from the team.

"Now, now, nothing to be jealous of." My lips twitch. "You know there's not a single visible hair on my nips. But I'll have you know, hairy chests are fucking sexy."

Do not look at Sully. Do not look at Sully.

Which is hard because I have a new appreciation for hairy chests since feasting on the man at my side.

"Hallelujah, there's a chance for all the non-body-groomers yet. Alert the press that the Wyoming Firefighter Bachelor of the Year committee are widening the pool," Remy hollers, his brows bouncing as he throws me shade.

"There's a Wyoming Firefighter Bachelor of the Year?" comes from Sully.

I shake my head and throw a packet of potato chips at Remy. "Ignore the asshole. He thinks he's funny."

Grinning, Remy presses his hand against his chest in mock outrage. "There is no *think, sweetheart.*"

I snort out another laugh at my friend. "Uh-huh, okay, wise guy." I glance at Sully, whose eyes are sparkling with amusement. "And there's *definitely* no Bachelor of the Year bullshit."

"There definitely should be," Remy adds. I snap my attention to him, willing him to be quiet, which is so not like me. "It would be great for charity. Just think how much more money the fire departments could raise in donations from *that* kind of event."

Just the very idea of Bachelor of the Year, especially for charity, would usually have me jumping at the chance to be involved. I have no issue with being in the spotlight, but fuck, I have Sully now. No way do I want to be involved in that kind of single dude meat market.

"Hey, Dean, you could talk to your brother, right? Get him to sponsor it or give it his seal of approval or something?" Remy says to Dean, who looks like he's mortified by the very idea.

"Uhm… maybe?"

Remy has a gleam in his eye, one I recognize as him getting carried away and totally on board with an idea. The thing is, it *is* an awesome idea.

And when multiple people in the room, including Alice, join in, completely in support of the prospect, I need to react.

Shit. Bachelor. Am I still a bachelor when I'm

dating? Does someone have to be married or engaged to no longer be one? I need to check.

Ignoring the excited, far-too-eager conversation around me, I tug out my phone and open up the dictionary app. Yes, I absolutely have an app downloaded to check out things like this.

I just have no idea how to spell bachelor, but this app is pretty good at figuring out my piss-poor spelling attempts.

"What are you doing?" Sully's leaning in close, his voice quiet.

I angle my phone to him so he can see as I focus on the third definition.

bachelor

noun

bach·e·lor ˈbach-lər

ˈba-chə-

3

: an unmarried man

He chooses to remain a *bachelor*.

Huh, so I'm officially a bachelor, then.

As I glance at Sully, trying to read his expression, Remy calls my name.

"So, what do you think?"

Shit, I completely switched off. "About?"

"A bachelor auction?"

"What the fuck is a bachelor auction, and what happened to Bachelor of the Year?"

He shakes his head at me, a small smile playing on his lips. "An auction could totally get more contributions. Plus, we thought that the bachelor who drew the highest bid could be labeled Bachelor of the Year. Dean's on board too. Right, Dean?"

Poor Dean still looks horrified, and I wonder how I missed all of *that* while looking at the dictionary.

"So, if I can get it off the ground for next year, maybe, are you in?" Remy pauses before adding, "But how awesome would it be if we could do it this year?"

There's nothing subtle about my wide-eyed reaction. What the fuck do I do?

This year…? Hell, definitely by next year, I hope to have locked down my relationship with Sully. In the next week if possible. And marriage…. Well, it's too soon for sure, but who knows how things will progress over the coming months.

Aware all eyes are on me and confusion is beginning to cross some of the expressions aimed my way, I clear my throat. "I think it's a great idea."

Don't look at Sully. Don't look at Sully.

"I can help in some way. Behind the scenes." An

idea slams into me, and I grin. "I can totally be on the mic. I can emcee the shit out of that." The spotlight and I are friends. That would be a blast and keep me involved while getting me out of the auction.

The looks of shock surrounding me have me rolling my eyes. "What?" Not going to lie, I'm a little defensive.

"Who are you and what have you done with the Hayes who would have created a whole promo campaign to make sure he got the highest bid?" Alice is scrutinizing me far too intently.

I deflect, saying, "I wouldn't even know how to organize a campaign, so I don't know what you're talking about."

Admittedly, my deflection is a little weak.

At my side, Sully shifts. My attention is drawn to him immediately. The asshole is barely containing his amusement. Fuck, he looks handsome, eyes practically sparkling with laughter. But still, he's being an asshole and clearly taking far too much pleasure in my panic.

I'm parting my lips, ready to tease him back, when the callout alert sounds. I make to jump up until I see Jacob stand and race toward the cubbies.

I'm not on duty, but fuck if the urge to race into

action doesn't have adrenaline coursing through my veins.

"Stay safe," Remy calls out.

I flick him a glance to find his gaze on Sully. I tense, wondering why he's staring so intently, then freeze when his attention moves swiftly to me. He studies me a beat before he arches his brow, a smirk forming.

I twist my lips and bite the inside of my cheek, narrowing my gaze a little. He huffs out a quiet snort, but it's not loud enough to draw the attention of anyone around us. Then the asshole bounces his brows up and down and throws me a wink.

Does the asshole know? In defeat, I sag back against my chair.

Sully and I need to have a serious conversation.

For one, I need to get this whole boyfriend label locked down. Then, we need to agree to tell people. I know it's kind of awkward for him, but I'm prepared to have a conversation with Rhys as soon as he green-lights it.

I just hope it's soon.

Thankfully, the callout interrupted the discussion about the charity event. It also breaks up the get-together and has us all finishing our drinks and leaving. Some of the group heads on to Jake's Tap, but my plan is to go home with Sully.

Sully beside me, we manage to get away without prying eyes. Once we're alone, I release a lungful of air. Not going to lie, I'm tenser than I realized.

"You okay?" All the teasing is gone from Sully's tone, so I figure he realizes I'm not quite myself.

"Yeah. I just want to get home."

He nods, two small lines appearing between his brows. I don't like that I've put them there.

We head back in silence, the atmosphere in the cab tense, and honestly, I feel the doors pressing in on me a little. When I pull up, we get out of the truck, and I lead the way, Sully a step behind me.

Once inside with the door closed, we head to the kitchen. Usually, I would have pounced on Sully by now. That's absolutely what I want to do. Every second we're together where I can't get my hands or my mouth on him is a moment longer than I'd like.

That I feel that way doesn't even worry me. I don't give a shit if I sound desperate or needy. It is what it is, and I'm tired of holding back.

"You want to talk about whatever's on your mind?"

I turn to face him, pressing my ass into the counter. I lean back, letting it support me. "Yeah," I answer honestly. Even more honestly, I add, "But I'm also worried you're not going to agree with me or want the same thing."

Moving to stand opposite me, Sully tilts his head, studying me. "How about you tell me what's going on, and we'll get whatever this is figured out."

"Are you my boyfriend?" I blurt out the question, my heart thundering as I do so. "That sounds a little too much like a conversation I had with someone when I was in the fifth grade."

His lips twitch. "You had a boyfriend in the fifth grade?"

"No." I shake my head. "I wanted one, but he turned me down flat."

"What an asshole," he says with a smile.

My lips begin to tilt high until I see his smile fade away, signaling that he's waiting for me to finish, or maybe it's him trying to figure out how to respond. How to say no. How to turn me d—

"In my head I've already been calling you my boyfriend, so if you want that label as well, I'm more than okay with that."

My breath whooshes out of me, and I move directly in front him. As soon as I'm in Sully's space, I wrap my arms around him, tug him close, and slant my lips against his.

The moment our lips touch, my anxiety melts away, replaced by the warm, steady beat of Sully's presence. His hands settle on my waist, pulling me closer, grounding me. The kiss is soft but certain and so fucking perfect.

For a few glorious seconds, the rest of the world fades into the background.

But then I pull back, the weight of the conversation still hanging between us.

We stand there, our faces close, his forehead nearly resting against mine. "We need to talk about this, about going public," I murmur, my voice barely above a whisper. "I know it's soon and that it shouldn't be a big deal, but I also know you have your doubts."

"No, not doubts. That's not it." There's a flicker of something vulnerable in his eyes. "I want to be up front with you," he says quietly, his hands remaining on my waist as if he can't let go.

"I'm kind of nervous you're going to say something like you're embarrassed about me." Just as I know my strengths, I know my flaws.

"I'm not embarrassed by you," he says so quickly that the sliver of self-doubt in my gut stills. "I couldn't be further from that. I'm proud of you, proud to be with you. You're incredible in every way, and it blows my mind that you even want to be with me."

He swallows hard, the words seeming to cost him something. He continues, "But I'm anxious about how my family will react—how my sister will react. My nephew. I don't want to cause tension or waves. I don't want them to think...."

"That it's wrong?" I finish for him, heart clenching at the thought of him feeling ashamed.

He hesitates, then nods. "Yeah. That I'm some old, overweight guy robbing the cradle. That's not what this is. But I don't know if they'll see it that way."

I let out a frustrated breath, sliding my fingers up to cup his face and brush the lines of worry etched into his skin. "Stop that," I say firmly, my voice taking on a strength I usually only use when out on a call. "You're not 'some old guy.' You're not just my best friend's uncle. You're Sully. You're strong, sexy, and—honestly? I like everything about you."

He blinks, clearly taken aback by my words, like he can't quite believe I mean them. But I do.

Determined, I hold his gaze. "I don't care what anyone else thinks. I want *you*, exactly as you are. The only opinion that matters is ours."

For a beat, he just stares at me, his eyes searching mine like he's trying to find some flaw, some reason to doubt. But when he doesn't, something in his expression softens, his grip on me tightening.

"I don't know what I did to deserve you," he whispers, his voice thick with emotion.

I shake my head, smiling softly. "You're exactly what I deserve, Sully. So, can we stop worrying about what everyone else thinks and just… figure this out, together?"

Sully lets out a long breath, then nods. "Yeah. We can do that."

CHAPTER ELEVEN

SULLY

IT FEELS like I'm in an alternate universe. It's the only explanation for the level of intensity and the sheer amount of shit talk and gossip I'm witnessing.

This knitting group that Hayes is a member of is… well, interesting. And while I have no intention of joining the group ever again—it took me just fifteen minutes and an epic fail trying to use needles to make that decision—it's been fun to watch.

Francine is apparently the queen bee of everything. I've heard her name mentioned a few times in the past month of being in town. She seems friendly enough in a severe kind of way.

There are also a couple of older residents, as well as Mr. DuPont, who I previously met. But what surprised me is that, as well as Hayes being here, there's also Ben—who apparently manages to drag his husband, the sheriff, along—and there's also a really nice guy called Greg.

It's definitely an eclectic mix, and it's not even a full house, as several other members of the group are absent for one reason or another.

I've already been put under the microscope by Francine, and I think I passed the test. I'm here simply as a new resident, checking out what the locals do, and as Hayes's friend.

Yeah, I suck and still haven't spoken to my sister. In fairness, she's barely been home. She's heavily involved in the tree-lighting ceremony/bash/festival (I have no idea what it's officially called), which I've discovered is a big deal in Collier's Creek.

All the locals attend, and they have stalls and live music. It sounds fun. I've already been roped into helping Hayes, who has a stall, sell as many calendars as possible. And no, I still haven't gotten a look at any of his photographs yet. It's on my to-do list.

I sip at my beer, grateful I chose the meet-up that took place in the bar. The group selects different locations around town. It's kind of sweet the way they spread their love around to the different businesses.

At my right, Ben leans over to look at my disaster

of an attempt at knitting. His eyes widen slightly before a slow grin spreads across his face.

"Oh, wow," Ben says, fighting to keep his tone serious. "This is… creative. I mean, I've never seen a stitch quite like this one before. Are you going for abstract or is this just… experimental?"

I snort, shaking my head. "If by 'experimental' you mean an epic failure, then yeah, that's exactly what I was going for."

Ben chuckles, leaning back in his chair. "Hey, no judgment. Knitting's harder than it looks, right? But, uh, this might be a record for most dropped stitches in a single attempt. Impressive, in its own way."

"Well, at least I'm good at *something*." I smirk, rolling my eyes. "Too bad it's not actually knitting."

"Don't sweat it," he says, giving me a playful nudge. "You should've seen Hayes's first attempt at this. Let's just say you're in good company. He tried to make a scarf once and ended up with something that resembled a really sad potholder."

I laugh, sneaking a glance at Hayes, but he's talking to Greg. "Okay, that does make me feel better. If Hayes can screw it up, then I'm definitely not alone."

Ben takes a sip of his beer, his teasing fading into

something a bit more genuine. "So, how are you settling in? You know, besides finding out you'll never make a living as a knitter."

I pause, considering the question. "It's been… interesting. I mean, it's a small town, and that's a bit of an adjustment, but people have been mostly welcoming. I think I'm getting the hang of it."

"Yeah? I've been here my whole life, and I'm still trying to figure this place out sometimes. But it's good, though, right? You like it here?"

"I do," I admit. "It's got this charm even if it's a bit intense with all the gossip and small-town politics."

Ben raises an eyebrow, a knowing smile tugging at his lips. "Speaking of gossip… heard anything about your nephew lately? Hayes mentioned something about him heading home at some point over the holidays."

He did? My heart skips a beat at the mention of Hayes and Rhys in the same sentence, but I keep my face neutral. "Oh yeah? I haven't spoken to Rhys in a while." *And Hayes hasn't mentioned a thing.*

Ben doesn't seem perturbed by me not speaking to my nephew often. He simply shrugs. "I don't really know Rhys all that well. He'd already left high school by the time I started."

My brows shoot high. "No shit?" I thought he was older than that. Sure, Ben is a damn sight younger than I am, but I'm aware he's a dispatcher at the sheriff's office. I'm also aware that the sheriff is in his forties. He's younger than I am, but still….

Questions threaten to singe my tongue, and I suspect that's crystal clear to the young guy at my side, whose his lips twitch as he says, "Go ahead and ask."

I glance around a little shiftily. Everyone seems engaged in some sort of conversation, so I keep my voice low when I ask, "So you and the sheriff. Have you been together long?"

"Over a year now." He smiles fondly. "Married since spring. Pop by the sheriff's department sometime, and I'll pull out the wedding album."

My smile comes easily. How can it not when he looks so happy? "I can definitely do that. And, uhm… when you got together, was that hard…?" I trail off, not knowing how to ask what I want to without sounding like a complete asshole.

"Because it's the sheriff or because he's twenty-one years older than me?"

Holy shit. My eyes widen.

Ben chuckles. "That look right there we got a little of, but honestly, there are more interesting things in this town to gossip about. Not that JD thought that at the time. Between you and me, he tried to resist, got it in his head he was too old for me or some sort of nonsense. It didn't take him too long to realize the error of his ways."

The sound of Hayes's laughter, free and joyous, interrupts us. A tingle of awareness shoots down my spine, and I can't help but turn to look at him. He's still laughing, all while his hands are working with his blue needles.

That sound—I want to bottle it up.

"I see."

I snap my attention back to Ben. His smile is soft and knowing. Unsure what to say and not wanting to question him or lie, I keep my mouth shut.

"Listen," he says quietly, "you've already listed off some of this town's faults, but the majority of towns-folk just want a happy life." He blinks, his eyes widening before he says, "Oh." He cuts a glance at Hayes. "Does Rhys know?"

For the love of all that's holy, that I'm so obvious is a worry. Perhaps I've been walking around with hearts in my eyes.

But since Ben is scarily intuitive, I shake my head. "No."

"Is that a 'hell no' or more of a 'not yet, no'?"

"The second."

The slight crease between his brows flattens out immediately at my answer, and he sighs. "Good. Hayes is the best, and like I said, I don't know Rhys all too well, but I don't think he's a dick, right?"

A huff of amusement escapes me. "No, he's not," I answer quickly, aware I've captured Hayes's attention. I don't even need to confirm his eyes are on me. I feel them as viscerally as I would his touch.

"In that case, you've got nothing to worry about." With that, he lifts the sweater he's knitting and inspects it while I finally look at Hayes.

Our gazes connect. *Are you okay?* He doesn't need to ask the question for me to know what he's thinking. It's there for me to read in his eyes.

I smile wide, hoping he can read me just as well. *I'm good.*

He bobs his head before turning to Francine, who asks him a question, leaving me to wonder why I didn't know Rhys is heading to Collier's Creek and when exactly we can expect him. I'm not even mad. Hayes knows I'm struggling with the idea of revealing our relationship. I suspect he didn't want me to freak out.

Rhys visiting does mean I need to suck it up. I've kept Hayes waiting long enough, and more than that,

I want to lean across and take his hand, press my mouth to his whenever I want.

We both deserve that.

I HEAD BACK to my place tonight. There are only so many times I can tell Abigail that I'm working late and keep getting away with it. At least this time I'm armed with a gift to put her off the scent. Well, "gift" may be a bit of a stretch considering what I'm bringing her is my fairly weak attempt at a dishcloth. I'd started making it at the knitting club and finished it later at Hayes's insistence while he cooked us dinner.

And yes, he helped me with the bind off.

Hayes promised me that he's made a lot worse, so as I pass it to Abigail, who's studying it as if it's going to turn around and nip off her nose, I grin. "Hey, I tried."

"Jesus." She looks from the yellow sort-of dishcloth to me. "How on earth did someone manage to get you to attend knitting club?" I don't have time to answer before she huffs out a laugh. "Of course Michael did." She chuckles and shakes her head. "That kid. I swear he's got a silver tongue."

While I happen to agree with her, once again the "kid" endearment makes me cringe. It's silly, really, and something I need to get over.

Rather than saying aloud that Hayes definitely has a silver tongue and the way he uses it on me is positively sinful—and that I love every moment—I respond, "Well, I can promise I won't be attending again."

She smirks as she looks at the dishcloth. "Your gifts definitely lie elsewhere, Tom." She picks up her glass of wine. "Have you got time for a glass and a catch-up? I swear it feels like I spoke to you more when you used to live in San Francisco."

Guilt shifts in my chest. Wine is probably a good idea, especially if I'm going to tell her about me and Hayes. "Absolutely. I'll top you up." I take her glass.

"Thanks." She stands from her seat at the kitchen table. "Let's go to the sitting room."

"Sure thing," I answer.

After pouring our drinks, I head into Abigail's comfortable sitting room and sit down on the couch, eyeing the tree in the corner of the room. "Shit, when did that happen?"

A Christmas tree is up in the corner, looking like something sparkly and merry vomited all over it.

"Just today. Though if I said two weeks ago, you'd probably have believed me."

I take a sip of wine rather than answering her.

Abigail rolls her eyes. "Is everything okay?" She's eyeing me with curiosity.

"Yeah, of course it is." Never better, in truth, but I don't want to say that aloud. Not yet, anyway.

"Hmm. Okay." She takes a sip of wine.

"Where's Larry?" I ask, pointedly ignoring her assessing gaze. Am I stalling? I am, and it makes me feel all kinds of pathetic.

Hayes is incredible. We both know that. I also know my sister wants me to be happy.

Car headlights flash through the window, and Abigail's face brightens. She quickly places her wineglass down before jumping out of her seat. "That's him right now."

She sounds far too excited that her husband is home.

"O-kay?" I drag out, peering over my shoulder as she rushes past me, goes into the foyer, and swings the front door open.

"Mom, hey."

Holy shit.

"Rhys, sweetheart." Abigail hugs her son hard while I stare on.

I really should have asked Hayes questions tonight about Rhys heading home. Getting distracted by his mouth before dinner looks like it bit me in the ass.

I stand when Abigail releases Rhys, and he steps out of her hold, his gaze landing on me. His smile is quick to form as he enters the sitting room, bounding my way.

It's been too long since I last saw him.

I hug him tightly, and despite the anxiety forming in my gut, I smile, genuinely happy to see my nephew. "How did I not know you were coming home?" I ask after we drop our arms.

I take Rhys in. It's been eighteen months since I last saw him—shameful when I think too hard about it.

"I was planning to come home just before the Christmas Bash, but I've gotta head overseas for a two-month project. So you get me now instead."

Abigail has since reentered the room, Larry at her side, both beaming with pride at Rhys.

"Well, this is a great surprise." It is, but even as I say it, my heart thumps heavily, sounding loud in my ears.

"Are you hungry?" Abigail asks.

"No, I'm good, thanks, Mom. I ate on the plane. I will grab a beer, though, please."

"On it, son," Larry says, squeezing his son on his shoulder before he heads to the kitchen.

"Make it two, thanks, Dad."

"Why on earth—"

The knock on the door cuts Abigail off. Rhys chuckles and makes his way to the door. He opens it fast and wide, saying, "Took you long enough."

"No fucking way." Hayes practically leaps into the foyer, hugging Rhys hard. "What the hell are you doing here?"

My pulse slows a little. Hayes didn't know he was coming. It makes me feel a little better and less like the rug is being pulled from under my feet.

"Surprise, asshole." Rhys gives Hayes a smacking kiss on the cheek. My smile comes easily as they joke and laugh, greeting each other.

"Here you go, boys," Larry says, holding out the beers.

With a chuckle, Hayes takes his beer and finally looks around. Immediately, his gaze settles on me. He's still grinning, that doesn't change, but there's a softening around his eyes when he takes me in.

I swallow as quietly as possible—even though Rhys is saying something to his dad—viscerally aware I'm too obvious around Hayes. Every time I'm in his presence, there's like an invisible string that has me staying close, always in his orbit.

How the hell am I supposed to keep that from my family?

I don't know if I can.

Maybe I shouldn't.

Fuck. Fuck. Fuck.

I take a step forward but stop dead in my tracks when I tune in to Rhys saying: "… not a chance I'm missing out on meeting this secret boyfriend of yours."

Hayes's brows jump high, and his cheeks turn red. He parts his lips and appears to stumble before settling on: "Uhm… what?" I'm impressed his gaze doesn't immediately snap to mine. Though from the look of discomfort in his shoulders, he's struggling not to look my way.

"Puh-lease." Rhys chuckles. "You haven't dated anyone, let alone had a boyfriend in so many years, but I absolutely remember the signs."

"But I haven't even seen you."

That's not a denial.

Which is immediately what Rhys jumps on. "Man, all I know is, I'm happy for you. And your voice and the way you've been clamming up when we've spoken told me all I needed to know. You've fallen hard."

My heart lurches in my chest, happiness blooming there, which is a million times better than the worry I expected to feel.

The thought pulls me up short.

I'm *not* worried. They're my family. And Hayes, he's something special.

5
P L F C

CHAPTER TWELVE

HAYES

ONE SECOND I'm surprised as hell and so damn happy seeing Rhys, the next I'm eating Sully up from across the room, wishing we were alone, and then I'm wondering what the fuck is happening.

How Rhys knows is beyond me, but more to the point, what the hell do I say or do?

It's taking every ounce of control not to stare at Sully in panic or a plea for help.

But it's no good. I have no idea what to do.

My gaze snaps Sully's way the moment he moves, and he eats up the distance between us. There's a look in his eyes that… okay, is sexy as hell, and I swear, the determination in his face is something I've never seen before, but fuck if I don't want to see it all the damn time.

Is he…?

My eyes widen, my eyebrows practically touching my messy hair.

Holy shit, he's definitely going to.

He's less than two feet away, and I have no idea where everyone else is looking or what they could possibly be thinking, as it's impossible to look away from the intensity in Sully's gaze. It's possessive and directed entirely on me.

I smile so wide that my cheeks ache, but finally, he's doing this.

"That'd be me. Hayes's secret boyfriend." He reaches for my hand and squeezes, wraps his arm around my waist, and finally glances at his family.

I follow his gaze with what I'm sure is a sappy smile. Larry's brows are high, and Rhys looks hella confused, his attention darting between me and his uncle. It's Abigail's expression that makes me pause. Her brows are dipped low, a look on her face I can't read.

My friend is the first to properly respond. When he says, "Holy shit…. Okay, a surprise, but I get it. I can see how you two could work so well," my shoulders sag. This is what I hoped for. Rhys has my back. He always has.

"Thanks, man." I lean in and hug him. "To be

honest, when we first met, we didn't realize the connection, you know?"

Rhys pulls away and shrugs. "However it happened, as long as you're both happy, I'll be cheering you on."

At my side, Sully releases me so he can hug his nephew. He mumbles something close to his ear before patting his back and stepping away.

And then I realize the room has become tense as hell as Abigail is standing there with that same odd look on her face. It's not exactly disapproving, but she doesn't appear especially happy either.

"Abigail?" Sully says.

Her attention travels to him, and her skin turns pink. "I forgot I'm expecting a call." A tight smile is sent our way before she turns and leaves the room.

We watch her go, and lead forms in my stomach.

"Right, well," Larry says, clapping his hands together. While he's smiling, it's obvious he's uncomfortable. Whether that's because of us or Abigail, I have no idea. "Let's go drink these beers and catch up. There should be a game just started."

He heads back to the sitting room and switches on the TV. We sit down a little awkwardly, me next to Sully with Rhys perched on the arm of the chair and wearing an expression I recognize all too well.

Before I can say anything, he stands. "I'll be back in a few." He leaves, and I absolutely know he's following Abigail.

Fuck. "Maybe I should go?" This feels super awkward.

Sully puts his warm hand on my knee, steadying it. That it was bouncing without me realizing isn't a great sign. I don't do well with confrontation, especially not when it really matters and with people I love and respect.

"If you want to leave, we can go."

I breathe a little easier at his words, at his inclusive "we."

"Nonsense," Larry says. He glances toward the archway his wife left through. "Abigail just needs a moment to process. She'll be okay."

A humorless laugh escapes Sully, drawing my attention. "Honestly, there've been a couple of times that I thought Abigail suspected and was even pushing us together." He shakes his head, and I hate it. Hate his uncertainty. His sadness. "I feel like an idiot for being so wrong."

Sully's sadness tightens something inside my chest. I squeeze his knee, offering what little comfort I can. "You're not an idiot," I murmur, but the tension around us is still thick, and no matter how much Larry tries to keep things light, Abigail's absence weighs on everything.

Our drinks are barely touched, and the basketball game on TV is nothing but background noise, especially after Rhys returns pissed off. Sully's normally relaxed posture is stiff, his hand resting on my leg more out of reflex than anything else. Larry keeps talking about work, about sports, and tries to involve me and Sully, but his words just float around without really landing.

I glance at the clock and realize it's probably best if we head out. We won't make this situation any better by staying longer, and Abigail clearly needs some space to process things.

"I think we're gonna get going," I say, standing up and patting Sully's knee gently.

Larry looks at me, his smile fading a little. "Are you sure? You don't have to rush off, really. Abigail just—well, she just needs time."

Sully stands beside me, his hand immediately finding mine. "Yeah, I think it's best. We'll give her some space."

Larry hesitates but eventually nods. "All right, but don't overthink this, okay? This is still your home for as long as you need," he says to Sully. "Let's have dinner tomorrow, okay? You know how Abigail is—she'll come around."

I nod, trying to believe him.

Sully and I make our way toward the door, and as we step out into the cool evening air, the tension starts to lift from my shoulders. Just as we're about to reach the car, I hear her voice behind us.

"Wait."

We both turn around to see Abigail walking briskly toward us, her face flushed and her arms crossed tightly over her chest. For a moment, I brace myself for the worst.

"Abigail," Sully starts, but she shakes her head.

"Just—let me talk, okay?"

Sully falls silent, and I squeeze his hand. Abigail looks between us, her gaze lingering on where our fingers are intertwined before she sighs heavily.

"I'm sorry," she says, her voice quieter now, almost strained. "I didn't handle that well at all. It's just… it was a lot to take in, and I wasn't expecting it. You have to understand, Tom—you may be my little brother, but you're Rhys's uncle. It's hard to wrap my head around."

Sully's brow furrows, but he stays quiet, letting her continue.

"And Michael, I've practically raised you as my

own," she goes on, her voice softening. "And now, to see you with—" She glances at me, her expression unreadable for a second. "Well, to see you together? Michael, you're like family to me too. So this is… complicated."

I swallow, my throat suddenly dry. "I get that, Abigail. I really do. But we're both adults now, and there's nothing complicated about that."

"I know you are." She cuts in quickly, almost as if to reassure herself. "I know. It's just… there's a lot of history here. I've seen you grow up, Michael. I've seen Tom grow up, be an uncle to Rhys. And suddenly, this?" She gestures between us. "It's hard for me to process."

Sully steps forward, his voice firm but gentle. "We didn't expect this to be easy for anyone, Abigail. But it's real. Hayes is not a kid anymore, and thankfully, I didn't really know him when he was. This is what we want. What *I* want."

Abigail sighs again, looking at the ground for a moment before meeting our eyes. "I know, Tom. And I'll get over myself, I will. I just… I need time, okay? This is going to take some getting used to. But you two—" She pauses, her lips twitching into a small, reluctant smile. "You seem happy. And I guess that's what matters."

I let out a breath, my shoulders sagging in relief.

"We are," I say quietly.

Abigail nods, her arms still crossed, but there's a warmth in her eyes now, something soft and familiar. "Okay. Well, I'll see you both tomorrow for dinner. Just… I'll try."

"That's all we're asking," Sully says, his voice lighter now.

Abigail takes a step back, rubbing her arms against the evening chill. "Drive safe."

"We will," I say.

With that, we watch her turn and head back toward the house. I glance at Sully, and he's watching her, too, a mixture of emotions crossing his face—relief, frustration, and maybe even a little sadness.

"She'll come around," I say softly.

Sully looks at me, his expression softening. "Yeah. She will."

We get into the car, and as we pull away from the house, I feel lighter than I have all night. There's still a long way to go, but at least we're moving forward. Together.

RHYS STAYS for the town's tree-lighting festivities. It's fun that he's still around. We don't get to see each other all that often, so that he's here now is awesome.

"Do you remember the one year when the sheriff caught us stealing all the mistletoe?"

I snort as I put the finishing touches on the display stand. "I totally blame you for that one." It's a little wonky, so I try to rearrange it again. It's no use. It looks like it'll have to stay this way.

Rhys laughs and adjusts the display stand so it's no longer sloping. Then he clicks in the last clasp on the sign that indicates the firefighter calendars are for sale. He steps back and nods. "Perfect." He glances at the boxes of calendars I'm hoping to sell. "How many do you have?"

"Not sure. These just appeared at the firehouse last week. I think the organizer was feeling overenthusiastic." There's a lot of boxes.

He chuckles. "Nah. More like confident that they know you're going to sell them all."

I roll my eyes, trying to keep my need to peacock on the down-low, but Rhys knows me too well and simply shakes his head at me.

The actual tree lighting isn't for a little while, but it's already getting busy. Practically all the town has shown up, including... "Holy shit, check out Geraldine."

Rhys peers in her direction, taking in her multi-colored poncho, and grins. "Is that Barkasaurus Rex? Damn, the mutt's still alive?"

I snort and look past Geraldine, my eyes widening further when I take in Mr. DuPont. Where's Sully when I need him? He needs to see this. Mr. D. wearing a Santa's hat is something to behold. Sure, it's not the elf's hat I teased him about, but I can barely recognize him or his wide smile.

Among the laughter and chatter, the bright, shining Christmas lights, and the holiday music playing through the speakers that the organizers have dotted around town, it's impossible not to feel the magic of Collier's Creek, especially during the annual Christmas Tree Lighting Ceremony.

"I'm glad I made it home for this," Rhys says from my side. "I've missed this place."

Picking up on the longing in his voice, I turn to glance at him, my brow furrowed. Rhys has an epic career in music management. Hell, the two-month work trip he tried to casually mention a few days ago is with one of the biggest-selling bands around. They're doing a tour of Australia and Malaysia.

"Hey." The familiar voice of my boyfriend

captures my full attention. I practically melt when I hear it, my focus turning fully on him.

"You made it." My grin stretches wide. Sure, he's officially here to man the charity booth for the fire department with me, so of course he was going to show, but since the awkwardness with his sister a few days ago, things have been a little tense. Not between us. When we're alone, it's easy for the rest of the world to disappear. It's just events like this that we're still navigating.

We have made some progress, though. We told Zoey and filled out some paperwork for HR disclosing our relationship. Cap was pretty cool about the whole thing and didn't even do a double take or question Sully's sanity.

"Of course." He lifts the two steaming takeout cups in his hands. "I even come bearing hot chocolate for you both." He passes one over to Rhys, who accepts it gratefully, and steps close to pass me mine. As he does, he says, "Extra marshmallows and a double shot of caramel syrup."

"Heck yes." I immediately hold on to the cup, lean into Sully, and press my lips to his.

A startled huff escapes him before he sighs into the touch. The kiss is brief, but it's enough for me to capture his flavor and know he's already drunk something syrupy.

I pull away, a throb of satisfaction pulsing through me when I take in his blissed-out smile. "You taste like sugar."

"Hot chocolate," he murmurs.

I chuckle, ignoring Rhys's "Honestly, I'm really happy for you both, but this level of sweetness is making me want to gag."

I flip him off and take a sip of my own hot chocolate, my eyelids falling closed as I savor the taste.

"Oh, and now my uncle's giving my best friend an orgasm. Brilliant."

I flip Rhys and his sass off again, only to snap my eyelids open at the sound of someone clearing their throat, and pretty pointedly from the sound of it.

Unlike me, Remy and Alice are dressed in their civilian clothes. What they are doing is staring at me and Sully like we've sprouted extra heads and…. *Oh.*

"Oh shit. I kissed you," I say not so quietly to Sully.

He meets my gaze and smiles. "You did. I think the promise of extra caramel syrup kind of got to your head a little."

I nod. His words make sense. "The marshmallows helped seal the deal."

"Uhm… while this is all super enlightening—"

"And ridiculously sweet and gag-worthy, right?" Rhys cuts in unhelpfully.

"Yes, that too," Alice says. "How long have you guys been holding out on us?"

I twist my lips while studying Alice and trying to get a read on her reaction. "Which answer will make you less mad?"

Alice's expression softens, and she tilts her head as a "you're such a doofus" smile forms. I know it well. "No being mad, more like settling a bet."

As I say, "Oh, in that case…," Sully says, "A what now?" sounding mildly alarmed, and I continue, "a few days before Sully started work at the firehouse."

Both Remy's and Alice's eyebrows shoot high at that.

"For real?" Remy shakes his head but doesn't look pissed off. "So, who won?" He turns to Alice.

"Uhm… I have a question." Sully looks around at us all. I helpfully just grin, leaving Alice and Remy to answer this one.

I've participated in more than a handful of wagers over the years—all in good fun, of course. Plus, there's usually enough cash involved to pay for a decent meal.

Alice sensibly doesn't make Sully clarify himself

any further. Sully may not have been our office manager for long, but he's already made his mark with his "take no shit" attitude. And yes, that means he's threatened us all with a safety talk at the local kindergarten already.

Give him six months and his threats will become even more hardcore.

"You and Hayes getting together." Alice shrugs. When Sully looks at her with surprise and maybe a little admiration, she continues, "Day one when someone joins the team, there are usually one or two —sometimes more—wagers started. One of yours just happens to be about getting hot and heavy with Mr. December here."

"*One* of mine?"

Alice squints, completely stepping in it. She glances at Remy.

He snorts before answering, "When would be the first time you called out for help after you got stuck in the snow."

Sully's "Fair" makes me chuckle. As does his "Honestly, I'm surprised it hasn't happened already."

I arch a brow at him, and he looks a little shifty when he throws me a grin and shrugs. Yeah, I've driven him to work and managed to get him home every damn time there's been snow on the ground.

Next week, though, we have a date for his first snow-driving lesson.

"So, who's the winner?" Rhys asks.

Admittedly, I'm just as curious.

Alice pulls out her phone, and I snicker when I take in Sully's expression.

"Jesus, how many people were in on this?" he asks.

Alice shrugs despite having the list on her phone. "We had an increase after the monthly session with the volunteers. But the winner was Marge."

"Aw, look, Uncle Tom," Rhys says super sweetly and with an emphasis on "uncle," which is something he's been doing a lot of despite not having called Sully "uncle" since he was seventeen, the asshole. "This is like your initiation into Collier's Creek. A rite of passage."

Remy chuckles. "Yep, it means you've been officially accepted. Another ten years and you'll be about ready to be considered a local."

I wrap my arm around Sully and dot a kiss to his cheek. "You hear that, Sully? There's no escaping me now."

He's rolling his eyes, but I know his pink cheeks are not from the cold. "In that case, it's about time I saw what the fuss over these calendars is about," he says, pulling away and eyeing the stall.

"Hold on." Rhys tugs out one of the calendars. "We haven't put one on display yet. Though, honestly, I think it needs to be coated or something. The number of sticky fingers it's going to get on it is going to be kinda gross."

I wrinkle my nose at the thought, but I stop short at Sully's "What the ever-loving fuck? You're on the cover?" He spins to face me, calendar in hand, the whites of his eyes clearly on display.

I glance at the calendar, nod, and shrug. "Yeah. It's not the same photograph as inside. In D—"

"December," Remy and Alice say in unison. "Yes, we all know you're Mr. *December*."

The urge to flip them off is right there, but there are more kids around, so I rein myself in. "Anyway, that image is a little more serious."

Sully looks at the front, his eyes still wide. I grin when he swallows. Yeah, it's a pretty awesome photograph.

He starts flipping through the calendar. "Just skip ahead of the others," I say quickly, much to the amusement of my friends.

Sully smirks, his gaze meeting mine. "I don't

know. It looks like you have some pretty stiff competition."

Sure, he's bouncing his brows and teasing, but I think the fuck not. "December," I say pointedly.

He chuckles and skips ahead. How it's possible that his eyes grow rounder is beyond me, but it's pretty great for my ego when my boyfriend is staring at a photo of me and looks like he wants to gobble me up.

His laughter fades, and he looks at me with heated eyes. "And how many of these do you have for sale?"

I shrug while Rhys, wearing a shit-eating grin, says, "I've counted fifteen boxes. Each box has a hundred, I think."

"Fucking hell."

A huff of laughter escapes me. I rarely hear Sully swear.

"Are you looking to purchase fifteen hundred copies, *Uncle* Tom?"

Sully cuts Rhys some side-eye before looking back at the open calendar, then at me. Amusement bubbles in my chest as I wait for his response, my brows high in anticipation.

"I'm considering it."

I snort, place my hot chocolate down, and tug Sully into my arms. "How about save your money and you can stick with the real thing?"

He angles his head, lips twitching. "But suspenders…."

I bark out a laugh. "They're mine. I keep them in the closet at home."

A mischievous smirk takes over as he says, "In that case, let's get all of these sold, except for this one"—he waves the calendar in his hand—"and then we can get out of here."

We ignore Rhys's over-the-top complaint and shudder. I'm fully invested in slanting my mouth against Sully's and capturing a kiss from him. While we don't deepen the kiss, it's not quite PG-rated, so far too soon for my liking, we pull apart.

"Deal," I say, a little breathless, and I'm sure my sappy smile matches Sully's. "How about you keep the hot chocolate coming and add an espresso shot in the next one to keep my energy levels up?"

We step apart as the first customer approaches, Sully shaking his head in amusement at me. "How about wait till we get back to yours and you'll have all the sugar you need?"

A little lightheaded and eager for the night to be

over, I set about getting every single calendar sold. The promise of any amount of time with Sully, naked or not, is all the incentive I need.

EPILOGUE

SULLY

ONE OF THE many things I learned early on is that there's no such thing as too much sugar when it comes to my husband.

I watch as he drowns a sliver of pie in whipped cream. There's so much of it, you can no longer see the actual pie on the plate. Grinning happily, Hayes spoons up a large bite, and like the sugar addict he is, he smears some of the whipped cream on the side of his mouth.

My chuckle is quick to come. It always is when I'm with Hayes. That didn't change in our eighteen months of dating or the three years we've been married.

Leaning in, I happily lick off the cream before kissing him firmly.

He sighs into the kiss, but I know if I don't pull away, this is going to get awkward pretty damn fast.

"You're incorrigible," I say, keeping my voice low. In the next room, our family is waiting for us. It's our turn to host Christmas Eve dinner. What we should be doing is dishing up dessert for everyone, but this man of mine is far too good at distracting me.

When I take in his expression, I melt a little further. A wide smile has settled on his lips, one that causes fresh butterflies to take flight in my gut. "What did I do to deserve that smile?" I ask, practically breathless.

"You just gave me a taste of my favorite." He arches a brow, his gaze fixed on mine.

We've played this game a time or two, and I'm here for it. Every single time. "Oh yeah, and what's that?"

"You know that it's you, sugar."

I do know, but I still love hearing him say it.

It's inevitable that I press another kiss to his lips. This time, he darts his tongue out and slides it just so against mine. I sigh at the contact, barely holding on to my restraint. Using all the control that I have, I pull back, whispering, "Dessert has always been our thing."

He parts his lips, but the fast tapping of claws on our newly tiled kitchen floor pulls us up short. We both glance over to the open doorway as Taz lollops inside like the soft brute of a dog he is.

"Oh shit." Hayes is upright immediately and rounding on our not-so-innocent three-year-old German Shephard who looks far too pleased with himself that he's captured one of Abigail's shoes. Wide-eyed, Hayes glances back at me. The plea in his gaze is obvious.

"Fine." I shake my head as I reach for some leftovers, lips twitching. "If he gets the shits, you're on clean-up duty."

"But you know the only way to get Taz to release shoes is with leftovers." He scratches behind Taz's ear as he looks at me with his own puppy-dog eyes.

"And who's fault, exactly, is that?" I arch my brow. There's zero snipe in my tone. Taz came to us as a rescue from Jayne a couple years back. He'd already had a weird fetish for shoes and had then destroyed more pairs than I wanted to count. It was actually Hayes who figured out that human food was the only way to distract our new family member. Whether a bowl of cabbage or a chunk of lamb, Taz was weirdly not that concerned beyond him clearly knowing it simply wasn't made for animal consumption.

And given that Hayes has since managed to rescue lots of shoes with leftover treats, I definitely can't be mad at him. But damn, our dog's stomach doesn't always agree with our bribes.

As soon as I call Taz's name, a slice of turkey stretched out to him, he drops my sister's shoe and races over. He immediately sits, obediently.

"He's such a con artist," Hayes says with complete affection.

"He seriously is." Amazingly, Taz does follow commands, and his obedience was something Hayes had worked hard on when training him. A good thing, too, as Taz is crazy strong. He also likes to hang out at the firehouse when we're both on duty, which is upwards of a full forty hours a week, since I ensure my hours match my husband's as much as possible.

"Is it damaged?" I ruffle Taz's head and glance over at Hayes as he examines Abigail's shoe.

He shakes his head. "No, thank fuck."

I chuckle at the genuine relief on his face. Out of all the shoes available to Taz when we're with family, I swear it's always Abigail's he goes for. "If we have to replace another pair, I think we should get shares at Abigail's favorite shoe store."

"It's because he doesn't want me to leave," Abigail says as she enters the kitchen.

Hearing her voice, Taz darts to her. She chuckles and squats down to give him a cuddle.

Hayes's smile is soft even as he rolls his eyes. "I think it's more to do with him being offended by the smell."

The glance she cuts him has him dashing away and me snorting.

"You're never too old, Michael," she says pointedly, her brow arching impressively high.

"Yes, ma'am." Sugary sweetness coats his words, and this time I roll my eyes even as warmth settles in my gut.

It took more months than I liked for my sister to be truly comfortable with my and Hayes's relationship. A combination of our age difference and seeing Hayes as a son had been difficult for her to adjust to. That and something about a really awkward situation between one of her former high school students and a member of staff didn't help her reaction.

At the end of the day, love won. That and her respect and desire for us to be happy.

She stands and eyes the plates we haven't finished dishing up. "Need a hand finishing up?"

"Nope, we're almost done." I pass her a couple of plates with pie on them, though, saying, "If you can take these, we'll just finish cutting the pie."

"Sure thing." Her smile is warm. "And if you can lock away my shoe, that'd be great."

Hayes chuckles and sets about wiping her shoe while I finally finish the job Hayes and I had come to the kitchen to do.

I make quick work of heaping the slices of pie on the multiple plates. When we bought this place a few years back, it had seemed a little large—at the time, unnecessarily so. But with the number of bodies crammed into our dining room at three different tables, it was the right call.

Drying his hands, Hayes sidles up to me, the scent of sweet cinnamon following. I glance at him, half expecting him to be drooling over the pie again; instead, his eyes are on me. Intensity burns in his gaze that I will never tire of seeing, let alone feeling.

It's the same look he directed my way when he first told me he loved me. That it was under a garland of mistletoe at the Collier's Creek Christmas Bash, not a couple of short months after us meeting, makes the memory even sweeter.

"When everyone leaves, that whipped cream is going to be coming with us into the bedroom." His voice is all huskiness and promise.

I clear my throat, easily getting lost in the visual. "That sounds messy." And so perfect.

His gaze sizzles. "Just the way you like it."

I barely contain my groan, and the thickening of my cock is so not optimal for all the obvious reasons. "You're so mean," I grumble with zero heat.

"And you love it."

"I do." I close my eyes when he presses a light kiss to my waiting lips. When he pulls away, I peer at him, loving the flush in his cheeks.

"Love you."

My smile is instant, as is the fresh swarm of butterflies. "More than coffee?"

A sexy-as-hell quirk of a smile is aimed my way. "Even more than sugar."

I huff out a pleased laugh, picking up three plates to carry out to our family. Before I leave, I glance back at him. "I love you, too, but that doesn't mean we can't see how sweet that cream tastes later."

Smirking, I walk away, loving Hayes's groan and the curse under his breath.

Hayes is absolutely my addiction. Nothing tastes as sweet as he does.

***

BE SURE TO CHECK OUT THE GRUMPY DEPUTY SHERIFF DAKOTA'S STORY IN ELLE KEATON'S THE MAP HOME, AND ALL OF THE OTHER COLLIER'S CREEK CHRISTMAS TITLES.

COLLIER'S CREEK CHRISTMAS

BONUS SCENE

SULLY

Hayes squeezes my hand. "So, officially the best Christmas ever?"

I smirk. "It's not quite Christmas yet," I tease.

"How can you say that with the number of elves we've counted so far?"

He's not lying. We've made a game out of it—forget *Elf on the Shelf,* counting how many elves it would take to overrun Collier's Creek is much more fun.

"True." I lean into him, appreciating the constant warmth that seems to radiate from Hayes. There's been plenty of snow lately, but the past few days have blessed us with nothing but clear skies and crunchy snow underfoot. Still, the cold nips at my cheeks.

Hayes grins at me, his eyes twinkling like the Christmas lights wrapped around the town square. "Now, how's that for timing?" He nods upward, and I follow his gaze.

Dangling from the archway above us is a sprig of mistletoe, perfectly placed.

I raise an eyebrow. "Did you arrange this?"

His grin widens. "I wish I could take credit for it, but I think it's just fate."

Before I can respond, the soft sound of sleigh bells rings out, followed by the first notes of "Silent Night" drifting from the band in the gazebo. The harmonies fill the air, wrapping around us like the warmth of a fireplace, perfect for the moment.

Hayes pulls me a little closer, his smile softening as he leans down to kiss me, slow and sweet, right under the mistletoe. My heart flutters, and when we pull back, he keeps his forehead pressed against mine, his breath warm in the crisp air.

"I love you," he whispers, the words quiet, but so full of meaning they stop me in my tracks.

I blink, my heart skipping a beat. This is it— we've never said these words to each other before, and hearing them now, hell if he hasn't timed it perfectly. I let out a shaky breath and smile up at him.

"I love you too," I whisper back, the words feeling as natural as the snowfall we've been waiting on.

Hayes's eyes light up, and for a moment, the world narrows down to just the two of us. The sounds of laughter, music, and Christmas cheer fade into the background as we stand there, still and wrapped up in the magic of the moment.

He kisses me again, this time more playful, a soft brush of his lips against mine before pulling back with a grin. "Now it's *definitely* the best Christmas ever."

I laugh, feeling light and giddy, the kind of happiness that lingers in the air at Christmas. "Okay, you win," I say, resting my head on his chest. "It really is."

We sway gently to the music, surrounded by twinkling lights and the hum of holiday joy. The band plays on, and when *All I Want for Christmas Is You* starts up, the crowd around us bursts into cheers, some even singing along.

Hayes looks down at me, his eyes shining with warmth. "Think we can find some cookies now?" he asks with a wink, his hand still tightly wrapped around mine.

I laugh, shaking my head but already smiling. "Fine, cookie lover. Let's go."

And as we walk through the town square, the

sound of Christmas carols filling the air, Hayes's hand in mine, my heart expands, fit to burst. This is everything I've ever wanted—him, the magic of the season, and a love that feels as bright as the twinkling lights around us.

BONUS SCENE

SULLY

Hayes's phone rings on the kitchen counter, and I glance at it. It's Jayne calling, which immediately piques my curiosity. We saw her and Steph just last night.

Hayes wipes his hands on a dish towel before picking up. "Hey, Mom, what's up?"

I lean against the counter, sipping my coffee, watching his face for any clues. His expression shifts from curious to… surprised? Then a smile slowly spreads across his face.

"Wait, seriously?" he says, shooting me a look. "Yeah, yeah. I'll ask. We've actually been talking about it for a while, so… I think it's a yes."

Now I'm *really* curious. I raise an eyebrow, but Hayes just grins and holds up a finger.

"Uh-huh, okay. We'll head over today then." He nods a few more times, says goodbye, and hangs up, turning to me with a look that I know means something big is about to drop.

"Well?" I say, crossing my arms. "What was that all about?"

He steps forward, hands resting on my waist. "So, you remember how we've been talking about getting a dog?"

"Of course." It's been a frequent conversation topic in the last year. We've tossed around ideas about breeds, rescue dogs, and even names, but we never quite pulled the trigger.

"Well, it looks like the decision's been made for us." His eyes are practically sparkling with excitement now. "Mom's friend works with a rescue group, and they've got a one-year-old German Shepherd who needs a home. His name's Taz."

"A rescue?" A swell of excitement and nerves bubble to life in my gut. We've talked about it for so long, and now the opportunity has just fallen into our laps. "Taz?"

"Yeah," Hayes says, laughing a little. "Apparently he's full of energy, just like his name suggests. Mom thought of us right away."

I blink, my heart already softening at the thought

of a German Shepherd bounding into our lives. "We're really doing this?"

Hayes pulls me closer, his eyes soft. "We've talked about it for ages. And it feels right, doesn't it?"

I nod, the nerves giving way to excitement. "Yeah, it does."

Later that afternoon, we pull up to Jayne's place, and I can hear barking even before we step out of the truck. Hayes looks over at me with a grin, and my stomach flips with excited anticipation.

"You ready for this?" He reaches for my hand.

"More than ready," I say, squeezing his fingers.

We head toward the yard, and as soon as we round the corner, I spot him—Taz. He's so much bigger than I expected, his fluffy black-and-tan coat shining in the late afternoon sun. And he's *definitely* energetic, bounding across the yard in a blur of fur and floppy ears.

"Taz, come here, boy!" Steph calls, trying to keep her voice calm, but there's no missing the affection in her tone.

Mid-run, Taz stops, ears perking up at the sound of his name. He tilts his head for a moment, as if deciding whether to investigate the new humans, then bolts toward us like a tornado.

Hayes crouches down just as Taz reaches us, and barrels into him, tail wagging furiously. Hayes laughs as Taz licks his face with wild abandon, his paws scrabbling against Hayes's chest, knocking him flat on his ass.

I whoop out a laugh.

"Okay, okay, buddy!" Hayes says, trying to wrangle him into a hug. "I get it. You're excited!"

I continue to snicker, watching the two of them, already feeling like Taz is meant to be part of our family. When Taz finally notices me, he bounds over, his tongue hanging out and his tail a blur. I crouch down, and he immediately nuzzles into me, as if to say, *Hi, I'm home.*

"He's perfect," I murmur, scratching behind his ears. His fur is soft and warm, and his big brown eyes look up at me, full of curiosity and sweetness.

Hayes's mom smiles from the porch. "He's got a lot of energy, but he's a sweetheart. I knew you two would be perfect for him."

"We'll keep him busy," Hayes says, standing up and brushing some fur off his jeans. "He's gonna love the trails near our place. And Sully will bring him into work, right?"

He glances at me for confirmation. I nod. "Yeah, once we get him trained for sure." I don't think the cap would appreciate an untrained German Shephard bounding around the fire department. Sure, Taz seems super friendly, but a dog like this needs a lot of training.

Taz seems to understand what we're talking about because he gives a deep bark, then leaps up, his paws landing heavily against my chest as he tries to lick my face. I laugh, ruffling his fur as I try to keep my balance.

"Looks like he's ready to go home," Hayes says, eyes shining as he watches me and Taz.

I grin, my heart full. "I think we all are."

As we load up the truck, Taz settles surprisingly well in the back seat, his head resting on Hayes's shoulder as we drive. The whole ride home, I can't stop glancing back at him, already picturing the life we're about to build with him in it—hikes, trips to the park, lazy weekends at home with him curled up by the fire.

When we finally pull into our driveway, Taz bounds out of the truck like he already knows this is his new home. He sniffs around, investigating the yard, while Hayes and I stand back, watching him explore.

Hayes wraps his arm around me, pulling me close. "Looks like we've got our hands full now," he says with a soft laugh, glancing at me.

"I think we're ready for it," I reply, leaning into him. "He's already part of the family."

As if on cue, Taz looks up from his exploration, wagging his tail as if he agrees. He trots back over to us, sitting at our feet and looking up with those big, trusting eyes.

Hayes kneels, scratching Taz behind the ears. "Welcome home, buddy."

And just like that, it feels like our little family is complete.

SULLY

"What's that look for?" I ask, grinning.

He glances at me, chuckling. "Remember when I mentioned Fred a while back?"

I pause for a second, thinking. "Fred… the moose, right? You said you'd tell me that story someday."

Hayes laughs, clearly glad I remembered. "Yeah, Fred the moose. Well, today seems like a good day for it," he says, indicating the forest trail we're walking.

I grin, giving him a playful push. "Okay, spill. What's the deal with this Fred?"

Hayes shakes his head, as if bracing himself for the absurdity of what he's about to share. And honestly, I know the story has to do with his mom,

Jayne, so at this point, anything could have happened. Jayne is awesome, but in just the couple of years I've known her, she's got herself into a few mishaps.

"All right, so this was a few years ago—when I was a teenager. Back then, there was this moose, Fred, who'd become something of a local celebrity. He used to wander around town like he owned the place. People would spot him in their gardens or just strolling down the streets like it was no big deal."

Amusement bubbles in my chest. I can totally see that happening in Collier's Creek. "So Fred was like the town mascot?"

"Exactly!" Hayes snickers. "But Fred was also a bit of a troublemaker. He was massive and had no sense of personal space."

My lips twitch at the idea of a moose having boundaries.

"One day, when we still lived in town, I get a call from my mom—she's half-laughing, half-panicking —and she tells me Fred's managed to get himself stuck between two trees in her backyard."

I raise an eyebrow. "Wait, what? How does a moose even get *stuck* between trees?"

"Right?" Hayes snorts, shaking his head. "Fred

wasn't exactly small, but somehow, he managed to wedge himself in just the right way that he couldn't move forward or back. So now, here's this giant moose, totally stuck, and of course, my mom decides she's going to be the one to 'rescue' him."

Laughter bubbles in my chest—Jayne in that situation easy to imagine. "What did she do?"

Hayes tries to suppress a grin, but he's clearly enjoying this. "Okay, so instead of calling animal control, like a normal person, she brought a *rope* and a bucket of carrots."

I burst out laughing. "A rope? For a moose?"

"Yup." Hayes is laughing too now. "She honestly thought she could *lasso* Fred or something. And the carrots? She figured she could 'bribe' him to cooperate."

"Oh my God," I gasp. "What did Fred do?"

"Well, Fred's just standing there, looking at her like, 'Lady, I don't know what you expect me to do here.' He's stuck. Completely immobile. And my mom is trying to coax him out like he's a stubborn toddler. She's waving these carrots in front of him, saying, 'Come on, Fred! You can do it!'"

I'm doubled over at this point, visualizing the scene. "Did it work?"

Hayes shakes his head, grinning from ear to ear. "Not even a little. Fred wasn't budging. He was just chewing on some leaves, completely unbothered by the fact that his enormous butt was wedged between two trees."

"So how did it end?" I ask, wiping tears of laughter from my eyes.

"Well, after about half an hour of my mom trying to sweet-talk this moose, I finally convince her to call animal control," Hayes says, his eyes sparkling. "They show up, take one look at the situation, and start cracking up. They managed to cut one of the trees just enough to get Fred loose. The moment he's free, he trots off like nothing happened."

I shake my head, still snickering. "And your mom?"

"Oh, she was *convinced* that the carrots helped," Hayes says, laughing. "She swears Fred moved because of them. But, honestly? I think Fred just liked the attention."

I'm still laughing as we continue down the trail, imagining the whole ridiculous scene. "I can't believe you waited this long to tell me that story." I'm curious where I can buy some fake antlers in town to wear the next time we head to Jayne and Steph's house.

Hayes grins, reaching for my hand. "I didn't want to give you all the ammo against my family at once. It's good to spread it out."

"It's a good job I don't scare easily, then." I nudge him slightly as we amble along, kinda hoping I get the chance to meet a friendly moose.

ABOUT THE AUTHOR

I live and breathe all things book related. Usually with at least three books being read and two WiPs being written at the same time, life is merrily hectic. I tend to do nothing by halves, so I happily seek the craziness and busyness life offers.

Living on my small property in Queensland with my human family as well as my animal family of cows, sheep, chooks, and dogs, I really do appreciate the beauty of the world around me and am a believer that love truly is love.

To check for updates head to my website:
https://beccaseymour.com
https://landing.mailerlite.com/webforms/landing/r9f0i4
Plus, join my Facebook group, which I share with the awesome Louisa Masters here:
https://www.facebook.com/groups/rommancewithbeccalouisa/

facebook.com/beccaseymourauthor

x.com/beccaseymour_

instagram.com/authorbeccaseymour

bookbub.com/authors/becca-seymour

tiktok.com/@beccaseymourwrites

patreon.com/BeccaSeymour

www.ingramcontent.com/pod-product-compliance
Lightning Source LLC
Chambersburg PA
CBHW051252210726
48287CB00002B/466